THE MAKING OF OKIE

THE MAKING OF OKIE

DONNA BARNARD

TATE PUBLISHING & *Enterprises*

Published by Tate Publishing & Enterprises, LLC
127 E. Trade Center Terrace | Mustang, Oklahoma 73064 USA
1.888.361.9473 | www.tatepublishing.com

Tate Publishing is committed to excellence in the publishing industry. The company reflects the philosophy established by the founders, based on Psalm 68:11,
"The Lord gave the word and great was the company of those who published it."

Book design copyright © 2009 by Tate Publishing, LLC. All rights reserved.
Cover design by Cole Roberts
Interior design by Joey Garrett
Edited by Amanda Reese

Published in the United States of America

ISBN: 978-1-60799-742-9
1. Fiction / Contemporary Women
2. Fiction / Romance / Western
09.07.06

This book is dedicated to the real Bo (you know who you are); to the people of Wilburton, Oklahoma, who, when I needed it most, generously shared their shade; and to Jerry, my technical advisor, best friend, and husband.

> For I know the plans I have for you, says the Lord.
> They are plans for good and not for evil, to give you a future and a hope.
>
> Jeremiah 29:11

CHAPTER ONE

Stepping from the truck into the stifling Oklahoma heat, Gwen Collins realized she was trembling. These past two weeks had done quite a job of wrecking her nerves, and this flat tire was the straw that had broken any resolve she may have had left. Oklahoma had gained notoriety by having record-breaking droughts in the past, and in Gwen's opinion, the summer of 1978 seemed to be striving to break some of those records.

She calmly walked to the rear of the truck and bent to study the flat. She rose, sighed, and looked down the dusty road. Raising her hand to shade her eyes against the sun, she slowly turned, panning a complete circle. There was nothing. Not a house, not a car, not even an animal in sight. There was nothing but a wide expanse of dried grass, drying trees, and even though it was only midmorning, heat waves were dancing off of everything in sight. Satisfied that there was no one to see her, Gwen began kicking the flattened tire. She absently kicked at first, and then, as if all of her anger and frustrations were finding vent through her foot, she kicked faster and harder with the side of her foot until she became winded and could no longer kick. She folded her arms on the top rail of the hot truck bed and dropped her head to her forearms. She breathed heavily but felt purged. At least the pain in her foot temporarily distracted her from the pain in her soul. Tears rolled down her already sweat-moistened cheeks.

"Why me, Dad? Why did you have to do this? Why did you have to put that silly stipulation in your will? Why did you insist on my living here? Why am I spending another entire year of my life in this godforsaken place? Why did you do this to me? Why? Why?"

Her anger began to rise again, and she was about to start another kicking tantrum, when she heard the sound of an automobile coming down the dusty road. She raised her head and saw a truck, crawling, weaving its way down the decaying road, unsuccessfully trying to avoid the many potholes.

Realizing that the truck was slowing to a stop, she hurriedly began mopping at the tears with the palm of her hand. The truck came to a halt just behind her, enveloping her in a cloud of dust. She felt it settle on her sweaty body. Vaguely, through the dust, she perceived a figure coming toward her. He was tall, muscular, and sunburned arms swung from the rolled-up sleeves of a denim work shirt. Beneath a wide-brimmed straw hat, she saw a shocking mass of dark auburn hair. Gwen noticed his ragged shirt and jeans, a pair of well-worn boots, the sweat-stained hatband, and she automatically wrinkled her nose.

He moved to the truck, never taking his eyes from the tire. "Looks like you have a little problem."

A real genius, Gwen thought but as calmly as possible said, "Yes." She didn't trust herself to say more, because she was still unsure of her voice. She certainly wasn't going to let this hayseed think she could be so upset by a simple flat tire.

Gwen had always been a fiercely independent person. After graduating from Long Prairie High School with the "Heavenly class of '67," which consisted of fifty seniors who were bound for great things, she went straight a fashion design school then to a position with a fashion merchandising company in Dallas. For seven years she had worked her way up the ladder, proving her worth through hard work. She was well liked and well respected in her trade and had recently been promoted to an executive position with T.J.'s Designs. T.J. was not only her boss but also her friend. The promotion meant the sports car she had had her eye on could be hers sooner. She had been saving a little each month hoping she would have enough to pay for at least half of the car and not have a large payment.

After she had gotten the job in Dallas, Gwen had stayed in touch with her mom and dad through cards and calls. She had tried to tell herself that she just didn't have time for a real stay. When she did visit, she was always working. She would retreat to her bedroom and work on designs for hours.

When her mom died three years before, she had forced herself to come home to be with her dad. During her stay, Gwen realized that her father was a total stranger. She returned to Dallas two days after her mom's funeral and a full week before anyone at work expected her to.

Family obligation forced her to call her dad once a week. After all, he was managing the ranch alone. She had tried, albeit halfheartedly, to get her dad to sell out even though she knew he wouldn't; knowing this, she offered to let her dad move in with her. He had once said that Twin Valleys Ranch was like a part of his body, just as much as his heart—he couldn't live without his heart, and he wouldn't live without the land. Gwen conceded and never brought the subject up again. She was secretly relieved to hear him say that he could never move off the land. Gwen realized that if her father moved in with her, they both would be very uncomfortable with the situation.

One evening her father had called and sounded so tired that Gwen worried about him. He talked about her mom and about how much he missed her. Before he hung up, he quietly said, "I love you, Gwen. Your mom and I both love you very much. Good night." Gwen sat for a while after he called. Her dad never called her. He had talked as though her mom were right there beside him. She dismissed the thought from her mind. After all, she had brought a ton of work home, and she had promised T. J. that it would be on her desk first thing in the morning.

The following day, Gwen received a call from J. D. Andrews, her dad's oldest friend and attorney. He told Gwen that a neighbor had found her dad that morning. He had quietly died in his sleep.

"It's ready, Miss Collins." Gwen was jolted back to the present by the soft sound of her rescuer's voice and the sound of the jack and the flat being uncer-

DONNA BARNARD

emoniously thrown into the back of Gwen's father's old pickup truck.

"Oh, I'm sorry. I should have helped. I was—How do you know my name?" For the first time, she really looked at this man. He had the most disarming blue eyes she had ever seen. Suddenly she was aware of what Oklahoma's humidity could do for one's freshness. She felt sticky, unbearably hot and gritty, and, strangely enough, a cold chill ran through her body.

"S-Sorry," she stammered. "I must look a mess." She absently brushed the front of her shirt.

"You look fine." He answered without looking up. "The reason I know your name is because I know that this truck is Will's ... or was. He said you'd come back after he died, but I never figured that you would stay for two whole weeks. This is not your kind of work, is it? I understand you're sort of a high-up muckity-muck in some kind of a dress factory or something."

As he spoke, he walked back to his truck, retrieved the tattered remains of a shirt, and proceeded to wipe his hands on it. Even through her cloud of misery, Gwen couldn't help but appreciate the view from behind.

"Wait." Gwen felt awkward as she trailed behind him.

He climbed into his truck. "How much do I owe you for your help?" Her eyes wandered down the forearm to the hand, which he threw over the rearview mirror. The hand was large, and the hair, which covered the back and the top of each knuckle, caught the sun and glistened a beautiful, deep auburn.

"You don't owe me a thing." His voice echoed from the interior of the truck. "Glad to do it." He adjusted the rearview mirror. "Well,"—he brought his hand to his hat brim—"I guess I'd better be goin.' Gotta go to town and get feed for my dog."

Gwen stood, nervously wringing her hands, thinking of her dad's, her, border collie. "I have to buy dog food also. Dad's dog—"

"Yeah, Pal...I know." He smiled.

"Yes. Pal. I have to find some dog food for him."

"I'm goin' into town if you want to follow. Fifteen miles is a long way on these roads if you're not used to them. They're not exactly the kind of roads a city gal is used to." Gwen wondered if he was being serious or snide.

"No thanks. I remember the way to town. It's not like I haven't been here before. I was raised here, Mr... . I'm sorry. I don't know your name."

"Bohanan, James Bohanan; but everybody around here just calls me Bo. I wasn't insinuating that you couldn't find your way to town, ma'am, it's just that now you don't have a spare tire, and these roads can be torture on tires. I just thought you might want me to watch out for you...but I guess not. Well, be seein' you." Nonchalantly, he waved a hand to her.

Gwen stood in the middle of the dusty road as he drove away. For a second time that day, she felt dust come to rest on her arms, face, and neck, and she blew hard to keep the dust from her mouth. She stomped her feet. *The audacity of that bumpkin*, she thought. *Work in a dress factory, indeed!*

She reminded herself that if she had been in Dallas no one would have stopped, and she would have had to call the auto club; that is, if she had had a car. She had never felt the need for one until just recently when she had seen that little red convertible—oh, she sighed inwardly, the little red convertible. Gwen thought about the man's lanky frame covered with steel-hard muscles, developed, she thought, not in a gym, but from hard work.

Gwen stood in the cloud of dust and wondered why Bo's comment bothered her so much. Gwen knew what she was worth. She could remain cool in front of sour-faced buyers. She had clawed and scratched for every rung on that ladder until she was just one below T.J. Good old T.J. If an employee ever called her Teresa, they had better be willing to look for another job. Still, she was a fair boss, kindhearted, a good businesswoman and a wonderful Christian, which was a difficult thing to be in the business world, but T.J. pulled it off with grace.

When Gwen had asked for a year's leave, T.J. had hesitated for only a moment. "Gwennie," she drawled in that beautiful, soft Texas voice, "there's a reason for this happenin' right now. I truly believe that God moves his people around just like pieces on a big ol' chessboard. We're exactly where God wants us to be at any given moment in time. And besides, it's only a year. Think about it. You're gonna inherit Twin Valleys Ranch. Honey, if it's anything like you've described, that's a section of pretty good land. Go on. Your job'll be here when you get back. We'll manage. It'll be hard, but we'll make out." She leaned back in her oversized leather chair and swung her feet up on the ornate mahogany desk. "I feel like you're supposed to be there for this comin' year, and there's no tellin' what you can get for that place when the year's over."

Staring down at the mottled, dirty feet in her shoes, Gwen wondered if it would be worth it.

Stubbornly she waited until all of the dust had settled; then Gwen sighed, climbed into the truck, and started it. Gwen smiled, remembering when her dad had bought the Ford truck in 1965. It was his first new truck. He had been so proud of it that he suggested that the three of them, Gwen, her mom and he go to town for ice cream. That was the first and last time her dad had gone out to eat anything. She remembered how proudly he had driven the sparkling green and white vehicle through town twice. He had the window rolled down and was waving at everyone he met. Finally they pulled into the local Dairy Queen. Now the truck was thirteen years old, a mixture of green and rust, but every time Gwen had asked it to, it had started. Sometimes it argued, but it always started.

Just when I was planning on buying that little red sports car, thought Gwen. *I had watched that car for three months and finally was about ready to take the plunge.* She took a deep breath. Resigned to her situation, she announced to the surrounding nothingness, "Guess I had better buy some people food to go along with that dog food. Looks like I'm going to be here for a while." She crawled up in the truck, pushed her hair back off her damp forehead, and started toward town.

Long Prairie, Oklahoma, was just a wide spot in the middle of a state highway. The highway went right through the center of the town, and the businesses, or what businesses there were sprang up on each side. As Gwen pulled into town, the first thing she saw was Guy's Diner. Then the Stop and Shop convenience store/gas station; Long Prairie Town Hall; the city utilities; a used car lot, proudly displaying two cars, six trucks (five of them 4X4's) a tractor and a topless jeep. Then came Fourkiller's Feeds, Leon's Barbeque, and the U-Haul-It lumberyard. At the end of town was a crumbling Dairy Queen where everyone made a u-turn.

As Gwen turned, she saw the white steeple of the Long Prairie First Baptist Church standing proudly in a grove of oak trees. Coming back through town on the north side of Main Street sat the post office; Bloomer's flower shop, whose signage was a pair of flowered Bloomers; Miss Hannah's Coffee Cup; Dave and Em's Barber and Beauty Shop; Kekso's Dry Goods; and the Liberty Theater. If movie watchers went to the theater when it was raining, they had better take an umbrella with them. Then came Andrew's Legal Services; Discount Pharmacy, the Lone Prairie State Bank, and another gas station into which Gwen pulled to have her flat repaired. After dropping the flat tire off at the station/bait shop, she proceeded to Jay's Super Foods, the town's one and only grocery store. As Gwen drove through the small town, sadly she noticed that where thriving businesses had once stood, there were now empty buildings slowly decaying.

The town had once boasted a population of over three thousand souls when the coalmines were in operation. But after the mines closed, many residents left, and those who remained were either still in Long Prairie or had descendents in Long Prairie. It was a close-knit community of around eight hundred people.

CHAPTER TWO

Gwen woke the next morning, fixed a pot of coffee, and began walking through the house as she sipped from her cup. Her dad was never one to clean house, and since her mom died, the housework had gone undone. She absently ran her fingers over her mom's piano and plowed a furrow through the dust. She looked around the living room, and her eyes fell on a picture of Christ praying in Gethsemane. Aloud, she said, "Okay God, You've put me here for a reason, and I guess one of them is to clean this house. Cleanliness *is* next to godliness." So the next several days were spent putting the house in order.

She was busy doing just that one evening when she heard someone pull into the driveway. She went to the door, propping the broom in a corner. Looking through the dusty screen, she saw Bo Bohanan walking toward the front porch. Pal ran to meet him, tail wagging, or wagging what tail he had. Pal had been born with only a stub for a tail, but he used it to the utmost. He was smiling a doggy smile. Bo stopped, leaned down, and gave a pat and a tousle to the top of his head. Obviously they were acquainted.

Slowly, as if he was aware that Gwen was watching, Bo raised his head, removing his hat. "Evenin,' Miss Collins."

He stood up to his full lanky height and proceeded toward the house.

Suddenly, Gwen was aware that her shoulder-length brunette hair had slowly been creeping from the pony-tail that she had hastily swept it into that morning. She had on no make-up, old jeans, and tennis shoes that had been found in the closet of her old bedroom. The shirt that topped this outfit was one of her dad's old work shirts.

Gwen began trying to coax her hair back behind her ears and brush some of the accumulated dirt from the front of the shirt.

"Good evening, Mr. Bohanan." Those beautiful blue eyes held her for a moment. "Come in, please." She held the screen open and stepped back in invitation.

Bo continued to stand on the porch. "I just dropped by to ask if maybe you were going to need some help moving your cattle."

Gwen's mouth fell open in surprise. "Cattle? What cattle? Move them from where to where? I have no idea what you're talking about."

He drew his hand across his face, and Gwen was sure she saw a hint of a smile flicker across his lips. "Your dad always moved the cows up to the summer pasture in April, and after that pasture dried up, he would move the cattle down closer to the house.

We've had a real dry spring and summer, so I went up there yesterday; and sure enough, the pasture is getting real dry, and the cattle have just about cleaned it up, cropped it as close as a nice carpet. You need to get them moved, and soon."

"I didn't know anything about any cattle. I suppose I will have to make arrangements to get someone to move them for me."

"I figured you didn't know about them, or you would have already had them moved." Was that a glimmer of a smile again?

"Mr. Bohanan—"

"Call me Bo."

"Mr. Bo, if you're laughing at me—"

"Oh, no, ma'am. I wouldn't laugh at you." He displayed the innocence of a junior-high boy.

"You *are* laughing." Her voice continued to rise. "You think you're so smart, plowboy." Gwen fairly spat the last word at him. She began walking toward him, wagging her finger in his face. He had a look of amazement as he began backing away. She retrieved the broom from the corner and continued her tirade. When Pal saw the broom, he headed for the barn. "You and your holier-than-thou attitude. I suppose you were born in a saddle with an innate sense of how to manage a ranch. Well, I was born on this ranch," she aimed her finger at the floor, "right here in this house, but my folks wouldn't even teach me to ride a horse. They were always afraid I would hurt myself. I couldn't help feed. I might get hurt. I couldn't help with any of the ranch work; I might get hurt. Then they die and force me to live here for a whole year of my life even though Dad

DONNA BARNARD

knew I had no knowledge of cattle or horses or any other thing that could help me cope with living here."

By this time, the two of them were out in the yard. Gwen continued her ranting and by now had her finger in Bo's chest. Seeing the shock on Bo's face, Gwen stopped. She took a deep breath, lowered her hand, and tried to calm her shaking voice. "I'm sorry." She lowered her head and stared at the dry grass of the lawn. She was ashamed of herself. After all, it wasn't this man's fault that she was here in this predicament. Gradually she raised her head and looked up into soft, understanding eyes.

Bo smiled and placed his hands on her shoulders and looked gently into Gwen's moistening brown eyes. "Your dad knew you didn't know how to run this ranch. He asked me several months ago to watch after you while you were here. He knew you'd have a hard time. He was willin' to help me; and for that I'm grateful, so I'm willin' to help you."

Calmer now, Gwen cleared her throat. "I have to live here on the ranch for a year before I will fully own it."

He lowered his hands and took a step back. "I know, Will told me he was gonna do that. We talked a lot. Your dad figured that if he just left you the ranch outright, you would sell it and return to Dallas without another thought. He didn't want that. That's how I got the Janway place, you know." He waved a hand toward the ranch to the east.

"When old Mrs. Janway died, the kids didn't care about ranching or the land. I bought it from them. Mr. and Mrs. Janway worked that ranch for forty years, and for what? Their kids, that's what. And what did the kids do? Sold it before the old lady was cold in her grave. Your dad saw that. He loved this land. His whole life was here. A life's work is right here." He swung his arms left and right. "Your dad loved you, and he wanted you to love this land as much as he did. That's why he did what he did. He was smart. He wanted you to learn a lesson in belonging to the land, loving the land, and appreciating God's bounty, just as he did."

Gwen was shocked at the way this man was describing her father. Suddenly she remembered the call that informed her of her dad's death. "A neighbor found him … " Mr. Andrews had said. She realized that Bo had been the neighbor. She swallowed hard, determined not to show the depth of her feelings. She cleared her throat. "Are we talking about the same man? Will Collins? The guy who never had a sentimental bone in his body?"

"Maybe he just never showed that side to you, or maybe he just grew that way as he became older and sicker. We've sat many an hour right here"—he pointed—"on this porch, talking. I knew your father better than anyone around here because I spent more time with him than anyone since your mother died."

"You certainly knew him better than I did." Gwen was painfully aware that these words, spoken by a relative stranger, had a ring of truth to them.

She felt a twinge of guilt, and again she felt the tightening of her throat as a tear welled up and spilled down her cheek.

"Hey now, don't start that. I'm leavin' if you're gonna spring a leak."

"No. I'm not going to spring a leak." Gwen smiled weakly. "I just feel really sad. I feel like I've lost some-

DONNA BARNARD

thing I never knew I had to begin with. I feel like I've been cheated somehow."

Bo gently touched her cheek where her tears had made rivulets in the dust on her face. She stepped closer, uncertain. His arms went around her and drew her nearer. She laid her head on his chest and let him hold her as she cried for her father, herself, and a relationship that they had never had.

Bo talked into the top of her head. "I miss him too. Your father knew that you were working all the time, trying to make a place in this world for yourself."

Suddenly, he drew back and held her at arm's length. He looked at her questioningly. "Hey, were you mad the day I fixed your flat?"

"Well, naturally I was a little upset. Why?" she asked, wiping her tears on her sleeve.

"I saw you in the rearview mirror. Looked like a stomp dance was going on."

"Oh, that. I was a little peeved when you said you thought I worked in a dress factory. I *don't* work in a dress factory. I am a fashion designer." Gwen heard smugness creeping into her voice and checked herself immediately.

"Oh, I see." He stood back and looked her up and down. Raising one eyebrow, he added, "Is this one of your latest designs? If it is, you'll be a lot better off to stay on this ranch and punch cows."

Gwen started to protest and then remembered what she was wearing. She looked up and saw a mischievous twinkle in Bo's eyes. He was trying to stifle a laugh, but eventually exploded into laughter. Gwen followed suit and began to snicker, giggle, and then began laughing. It was the first time since her father's death she felt like laughing.

CHAPTER THREE

Gwen's lessons in ranching started the next day. Bo was on her front porch at six a.m. Gwen hadn't gotten out of bed yet, and Bo was ready to go move cows from the summer pasture.

"Hey, Dallas," he yelled, pounding on the door, "you'd better get up. We have work to do."

Startled out of a sound sleep, Gwen couldn't remember where she was for a moment. Then she remembered that she had agreed to help move cattle today.

"Just a minute," she answered, climbing from her bed.

The morning was cool, and a breeze played with the bright yellow curtains in the bedroom that had been Gwen's as a child. Although she could have slept in any room in the house, she still came to this room to sleep because this was where she felt safe. She had many happy memories that were entwined with the smells and tastes of the house, but the happiest were right here in her room.

Padding barefoot to the front door, she unlocked it. "Wait a minute then let yourself in," she said through the closed door. Quickly she made her way back down the hallway. "Okay," she shouted. "Come on in."

She rushed back to the bedroom to get dressed. She heard him enter the front door.

"Hey, where's the coffee?"

"I'm sorry. I don't have any made. If you know where it is, help yourself. I could use a cup myself."

Gwen opened her closet and went through her clothes, looking for something suitable. *What does one wear to move cattle?* she wondered. Finally, she settled on khaki-colored pants and a sleeveless pink blouse. She knew that the day would quickly warm up to one of Oklahoma's famous humidity-plagued August days. She hurriedly washed, pulled her hair up in a ponytail, and brushed her teeth. She had wanted to look nice for Bo today, but there was no time.

She slid her feet into pink sandals and picked up her sunglasses on the way out the door of her bedroom. Bo was standing in the kitchen.

"Well, good morning. I hate to wake you from your beauty sleep, but we need to get started."

She looked around the kitchen, hoping for at least a cup of the coffee she smelled but hated for Bo to be delayed any further.

"I'm ready, I guess," she answered.

Bo was reaching for his straw hat, which was laying on the kitchen table. "Around here we have to get an early start, 'cause if we don't, the heat will be so stifling we can't get the cattle to move. When it's hot, they don't like to move any more than people do."

"Just how many cows are we talking about?" Gwen felt uneasy, and her eyes betrayed her feelings.

"Oh, I'd say a hundred head of momma cows, and if the bulls did their jobs well, a hundred baby calves."

"Two hundred cows!" Gwen was shocked. "Two hundred?"

"Yep, but I'm not leavin' here till we have a cup of this coffee I made." He laid his hat back on the table, rose, poured each of them a cup of coffee, and settled back down. "Do you know where your dad kept his ranch books? I know he had a good set of books, 'cause he's the one who taught me how to take care of the paper end of ranching." Bo sipped on his cup of coffee.

"I'm sorry. I don't know, but I will probably find them while I'm cleaning. I know where he kept his important papers, so probably his ranch books are there too. Why? Do you need to look them over?"

"Nope, but you do. You can learn quite a bit about what's to be done on a ranch just by looking over a good set of ranch books." He rose and stretched. For the first time, he noticed how Gwen was dressed. "Is that what you're wearin'?"

"Yes, what's wrong with it?" Gwen looked down at her clothes.

"Nothin,' I guess; I've just never tried riding a horse in sandals before."

"Mr. Bohanan, I doubt seriously if you have ever done anything in—" Gwen did a double take. "What do you mean ride a horse? We're riding a horse? You mean we have to ride a horse to do this thing to these cows?"

"No, I mean that we are going to have to ride *two* horses to do this thing with these cows."

"I don't know how to ride a horse. I don't even own a horse."

"Oh, yes you do. I have your dad's mare over at my place. She's carrying a foal. Her first. Your dad wanted her watched, so I offered. Plus, I would like to be around when she has this foal. I have an interest in it too."

"And what would your interest be, Mr. Bohanan?"

"I own the stud."

"Ah, yes. You would," she answered under her breath.

"Huh? What did you say?"

"I was just talking to myself. Are you sure that she will be all right? I wouldn't think a pregnant mare should be ridden hard."

"We're not going to be riding hard. She'll be fine."

"Not riding hard! Aren't we going to be driving cattle?"

"You've seen too many western movies, Dallas."

Frowning, she turned and cocked her head but let the remark slide.

He rose, placed his wide-brimmed hat on his head, and turned to her. "Well, if we're going, let's go, Dallas."

She placed her arms on her hips, hoping that this action would make her appear sterner. "Will you please not call me that?"

"Call you what?"

"Dallas."

"When you stop acting like you're from Dallas and start acting like you're from Oklahoma, I'll stop calling you Dallas." He turned and swaggered through the door.

Gwen went back to her bedroom and replaced the sandals with a pair of running shoes. She didn't own a pair of cowboy boots. There was never any reason to own a pair.

As she stepped outside, Pal was waiting for her. He was grinning his doggy grin and wagging his partial tail until it looked as if it hurt. "Are you excited, boy? Yeah, I'll bet you are. It's been awhile since you helped round up cattle, huh?" Still smiling at the dog, she asked, "Is Pal going with us?"

"Sure he is. Next best thing to a good foreman is a good stock dog, especially if you're gathering cattle for the first time." He grinned sheepishly and shuffled off toward his truck.

Gwen took a deep breath. She was determined not to let this man get to her. She walked stiffly to the truck and climbed in. She sat primly with her hands folded in her lap. She kept her eyes averted, not wanting to look at Bo. In the rearview mirror she could see Pal in the bed of the truck. He was so excited he was pacing from one side of the bed to the other, panting. In spite of herself, Gwen had to smile at his enthusiasm.

"I don't know whether or not to mention this, but this sun gets awfully hot, and if you're prone to sunburn, you may need a hat and some longer sleeves."

Bo appeared not to notice her mood or at least not to be bothered by it.

She turned and looked at him, sticking her chin out. "I don't sunburn. Thank you for your concern though." After she said it, she felt that she needed to bite her tongue.

DONNA BARNARD

Bo shrugged and mouthed, "Okay." He started the truck, and it lurched into action.

Gwen and Bo drove in silence to the Janway place, which was only a short distance to the east of the Collinses' place. As the truck bounced into Bo's driveway, an intake of breath made Bo turn and look at Gwen. "What is it?"

"The place really looks nice," she answered, a look of awe on her face. "I can't ever remember it looking better, or even this good, as a matter of fact."

"I did it for the old Janways. They deserved it."

Bo stopped the truck and slid from the seat. His border collie, Roxie, came running. Pal jumped from the bed of the truck, and the two dogs exchanged greetings.

Bo spoke through the open window, "If you want, you can wait here until I get the horses saddled."

Stubbornly, Gwen refused and fell in behind him. "I'll help you saddle the horses." This was a decision that she knew she would soon regret. It had been years since she had been around a horse and never without her father telling her to be careful. She had never saddled a horse and knew only that the saddle went somewhere in the middle of the back of a horse. How it stayed there was a mystery. Her dad had always done that sort of thing.

"Fine, suit yourself." He was already headed toward the barn.

As she started through the gate behind him, Gwen's resolve began to fade as a shiny black horse came walking through the barn door. He gave a low nicker of recognition.

Bo strode up to the horse and gave him a chuck

under the bottom lip. "Beautiful, isn't he? This is Silver Wings. Wings, this is Dallas. She is our neighbor and the owner of that mare that you've been trifling with."

A stallion! Memories of a stallion that her dad had once owned came rushing into Gwen's mind. Her mom had been so afraid of the stallion that Gwen wasn't allowed in the pasture as long as the stallion was on the place. Her dad had promised Gwen's mom that as soon as the stallion had bred his mare, Nubbin, he would have him neutered. But when the mare was bred, her dad didn't have the heart to have him neutered, so he sold him. Gwen never saw the stallion again but was allowed to see the foal when it was born, a miniature duplicate of Nubbin.

But what Gwen remembered most were broken fences, gates torn down, a smashed barn door, and Mr. Janway making plans to sue her dad for what the big stallion had done to three of his finest mares. Her dad just laughed and told her mom that he was going to charge Mr. Janway a stud fee because the old geezer had probably turned the stallion in with his mares to begin with.

Gwen felt her heart pounding and found it difficult to breathe; the tightening of her throat scared her. She was afraid that she would pass out simply from fright. She tried to disappear behind Bo, but he reached around and took her by the wrist. "What's the matter? Are you afraid of Wings?"

"Of course not." She squeaked and cleared her throat. "He's very pretty," she answered from behind Bo.

"Pretty! He's not pretty. He's beautiful. He's perfect." Bo's hands were caressing the horse, and Gwen

DONNA BARNARD

could see that Bo loved him and had a lot of pride in the horse.

"Isn't he mean?" she asked, still trying to unobtrusively hide behind Bo.

"Mean? No, Wings isn't mean. He's one of the calmest stallions you'd ever want to be around."

"He's the *only* stallion I've ever been around."

Bo stared at her incredulously. "You mean to tell me that you were raised on a ranch, and you were never around a stallion? Your dad told me that he owned one of the best studs around here at one time."

"He did but that time was very short, and I was never allowed to be this near the horse. He was kept in the barn or in the lot next to the barn. I told you that my parents were always afraid that I would get hurt in some way."

"Well, you don't have to worry about Wings." Bo walked over to stand beside the horse, rubbing him all the while. "Your horse is in here. Come look." Bo motioned with his head toward the interior of the barn.

Gwen made a wide circle around Wings and tentatively stuck her head in the dimly lit barn. When her eyes became adjusted to the dimness, she could see in a corner stall a graceful sorrel mare. There was a sheen to her coat that made her almost luminescent. "She looks like Nubbin." She remembered that Bo probably wouldn't know who Nubbin was. "Nubbin was a mare that dad had when I was a child," Gwen explained.

"Your dad told me all about Nubbin, and Nubbin's filly, and Nubbin's filly's filly. This mare has a reason to look like Nubbin. This is Nubbin's granddaughter."

"Really." Suddenly Gwen once again felt cheated

and ashamed that this man knew more about her father and the ranch than she did.

Bo saw the look. "You feelin' sad about your dad again? You shouldn't. Your dad was a fine, hard-workin' man. He was proud of you because you are a fine, hard-workin' woman. Your dad liked what he did, and you like what you do. What's wrong with that? You two just didn't like the same things."

"But I didn't have a chance to like ranch life. I was always *protected*. I may have liked ranch life and never have left here if I had been given a chance to like it."

"Well," observed Bo, trying to change the mood, "you're gonna get your chance. You can begin finding out today whether or not you like ranch life. Come on."

He strode off toward the tack room with Gwen innocently following behind.

Bo started explaining the care and grooming of a working horse as they entered the tack room. "Before you ride a horse, you have to clean their feet and brush 'em real good."

"Why?" Gwen turned and looked at Wings's hooves. His feet appeared to be perfectly clean to Gwen.

"Clean their feet to protect their feet. Pea gravel can cripple a horse for several weeks if it decided to do something like work its way through a hoof. How would you like walking, carrying a heavy load, with a rock in your shoe?"

Bo didn't seem to notice, but by this time, Gwen *was* carrying quite a load. He kept handing her all sorts of things as they walked around the tack room. She reminded herself to check to see if there was a rock in her shoe.

"Well, I guess that just about does it. You can help me get them ready."

"I assumed I was already helping." Hearing the sarcasm in her voice, Bo turned.

"Gosh, I'm sorry. I didn't realize I had given you quite so much stuff. Here let me carry that halter." With that he grabbed a green halter and lead rope and walked from the tack room, leaving Gwen with everything else. Haltingly, she made her way through the door to find Bo, leaning against the wall of the tack room right outside the door. He grinned and took an armload of things from her.

Bo took off toward Wings. Gwen followed. "Okay, each horse has to be haltered before we begin. This is a halter." He held a halter up high so that Gwen could see it plainly. He turned to Wings. "Come here, boy." Wings walked to Bo.

Gwen was becoming upset with Bo's antics. "Bo, if you are going to show me how to do this, please proceed and drop the professor junk."

"Yes, ma'am." He straightened and began to show Gwen how to put a halter on a horse.

"Now," he said, "can you manage to put the halter on your horse?"

Gwen was still standing, watching as Bo went through the steps to put a halter on. She was still holding brushes, a halter, and things for which she had no name.

"Here let me have some of that stuff, and you can have both hands to manage Apple."

"Apple? You didn't tell me that was her name. That's a nice name. Strange but nice." Bo took the assortment of things from Gwen and left her with only a halter.

He started for Apple's stall. *At least he's going with me,* Gwen thought. *He's not just going to turn me loose and assume that I can do this halter thing after seeing it done only one time.*

"Why did Dad call this horse Apple? That's an odd name for a horse."

"You won't think it's so strange when you look at her rear. Her butt looks like a big red apple, all shiny and ripe."

"Oooo, I can't wait for that," Gwen answered, screwing up her face.

Bo opened the door to the stall and walked in with Apple. "Come on in here, and let's see what you can do. Hey, girl," he said to Apple. He gently laid his hand on her shoulder, and she seemed to calm at his touch. "She's a good girl." He crooned in a quiet monotone. Gwen guessed the voice was what was calming the mare. *I could use a little of that calming myself,* she thought. She could feel her heart pounding.

"Okay, Dallas. Do you remember what I showed you?"

Gwen raised the halter, and in doing so, two of the metal pieces touched and clanked. Apple threw her head backward.

Immediately, Bo began the calming process again. "Around all kinds of livestock, horses, cows, sheep, goats, whatever, you have to go slow and easy. That's the key. Slow and easy." The whole time Bo was talking, he was rubbing Apple. "You're a stranger, and livestock don't like strangers, but the only way you're going to *not* be a stranger is to be around them. Did that make any sense at all?"

"Strangely enough, yes; it did make sense."

Gwen held the halter up toward Apple's head, and she again moved backward. Gwen tried this maneuver three more times with the same results. On the fourth try, Gwen began the singsong talking to Apple. "Hi, Apple. We are going to become really good friends. My name is Gwen. Although some folks don't seem to know that," she cut her eyes toward Bo, who turned his eyes to the ceiling in mock innocence.

"Whether you realize this or not, I am your owner." The monotone seemed to be working. Apple appeared to be calming down. *This is a breeze*, Gwen thought. She couldn't see the smile that had crept across Bo's face. She turned to him, and his stony countenance returned. "Am I doing okay?" she asked, raising her eyebrows in question.

"You're doing just great. I would have never believed that you were doing this for the first time. You're a natural." Gwen wondered if he were being sarcastic or was actually as stunned as he seemed to be.

Gwen lifted the halter around Apple's head to find that her five-foot-five frame wouldn't stretch to reach the buckle to fasten it. Bo reached to help, but Gwen shook her head, indicating that she didn't want help. "No, thank you. I'll manage." She dropped her voice to a monotone again. "Listen, Apple. I am not tall enough to reach this buckle, so you will just have to lower your head for a second. I know it might hurt your neck a little, but if I have to kick you in the shins, it will hurt you more." Gwen thought she heard Bo chuckle. Presently, Apple lowered her head enough so that Gwen could buckle the halter. What Bo didn't see was how white Gwen's knuckles were from pulling down on the halter.

"Well, I'll be," he said, scratching his head. "I wouldn't have believed that if I hadn't just seen it with my own eyes. You ladies will make quite a team. Yes, sir, that was something." He walked from the stall, wagging his head from side to side.

After Bo had explained to Gwen how to brush a horse, she began. She used the same slow soft voice that she had used to halter the mare, and Apple stood quietly while Gwen brushed her all over. Gwen had to locate a feed bucket to stand on to brush the middle of the back, but in a short time, the brushing was done. By the time she was finished brushing Apple, Gwen saw that Bo already had Wings saddled and tied to a fence post. Bo was walking toward Apple with a saddle and blankets. "I think I had better do this for you. Sometimes these saddles can get heavy for me, and I know that you can't throw this saddle up on her back from the bottom of that bucket."

He placed the saddle on the ground so that it rested on the saddle horn and placed the blankets on Apple's back. Everything went smoothly; he chuckled as he fastened the girth. "Pretty soon we'll have to let this out, momma. You'll be getting' too fat for it to fit." Are you watching this, Dallas? The next time you get to do this by yourself. You're so good with this horse, she'll probably lie down and let you put this rig on her."

Bo continued to talk, and Gwen let her mind wander. She watched the ease with which he handled the horse. His sure manner was a wonder to watch. As Gwen stood and held the lead rope, her eyes started wandering also. She started with Bo's feet and slowly, deliberately, slid up his body. He moved easily around the horse, bending and reaching for the cinch and breast harness. He explained what each piece was called and its function. Gwen was aware that he was speaking, but the warm sun and the closeness of his body made her feel light-headed and giddy. She thought about the fondness in his voice when he spoke of her father. She thought Bo was probably a gentle man for all his gruffness and impudence, and beneath his brazen exterior there was a caring person, an understanding man—the kind of man she had fantasized about when she was a girl of thirteen. Unfortunately, the type of man Gwen had dreamed about never seemed to be the type of man who was interested in her. She wanted a boy who was a Christian, but the boys who went to their church were not the steady, down-to-earth guys she wanted.

"There you go," he said as he took the lead rope from Gwen's hands. "All you need now is a hackamore," he smiled down at her, and becoming conscious of her thoughts from a moment ago, she blushed and quickly averted her eyes, afraid that he might read her thoughts.

"A what?" It sounded as if he had told her she needed a tree.

"A hackamore. Like a bridle with reins, you know." He was being impish again.

He unbuckled the halter and lowered it to Apple's neck and placed the hackamore over her head. "Do you think you need a boost?"

"You mean we're ready to go?" The old familiar fear came rushing back, and Gwen could feel the tightening in her throat and her heart pounding.

"Yep. You always mount a horse from the left and get off from the left." He held his hand out to take hers and give her some help getting on Apple. "Put you left foot in the stirrup and swing your right foot over and put it in the stirrup on the other side. Then, Dallas, to quote someone, you'll be a-horseback."

Gwen lifted her left foot as high as she could and still fell short of being able to reach the stirrup. She turned to Bo and said apologetically, "I guess I'm too short."

"Maybe you're not too short. Maybe Apple is too tall. I'll give you a hand up. Put your left foot right here." He laced his fingers and indicated his cupped hands. He bowed down so Gwen could easily place her foot in his laced fingers.

She was very self-conscious as she placed her foot into his strong hands. *What if he can't lift me?* But Gwen soon knew she had nothing to fear because it seemed she was nothing for him to lift, and she was up on Apple's back in no time. She looked down. It must have been twenty feet to the ground. She was certain that should she fall she would surely be killed.

"Let me adjust those stirrups to fit." He began to loosen and refit. "You're not quite as tall as your father. He was the last person to ride this saddle. Come to think of it, he was probably the *only* person to ride this saddle." Gwen felt a sudden rush of pride as she reached down and gently touched the swells of the saddle, the one place she was certain that her father had touched. Bo noticed her movements, and nodded, silently approving. Then he walked over to Silver Wings.

Gwen wanted to ask Bo if he would lead Apple for her, but her pride wouldn't allow her to do that. She watched from her airy perch as he confidently swung

DONNA BARNARD

himself into his saddle and arranged his body to fit the seat more comfortably.

"Let's go." He swung the big stud horse toward the gate and left Gwen sitting there, not knowing what to do. He turned, saw that she was still not moving, and returned, bringing Wings alongside Apple. "Oh, yeah, you have to let Apple know when you want to go and where you want to go." He gave her a quick lesson in steerage of a horse, which to Gwen seemed the opposite of what it should have been.

Apple started to walk slowly toward the gate, and Gwen's heart could have been heard in the next county if anyone was listening. With each step, she felt that she would fall off. She grabbed the horn more tightly and clung to the sides of the saddle with her legs. How could anyone ever learn to ride like the cowboys she had seen in movies? They always made it look so simple. Gwen had always imagined herself riding out through a pasture of green grass as fast as her horse could carry her. And always the wind was whipping through her hair and the sun was glinting off each blade of grass. She smirked. *Here I am trying with all my might not to fall off of this horse, traveling at the speed of a hyperactive snail. How can I ever pretend to move cattle today? I first need three months of riding lessons... and my fanny hurts already.*

Gwen began to relax a little, becoming accustomed to the lumbering of the mare as they made their way across the pasture. Bo told Gwen that they would come out on the county road near her own ranch. The sun was becoming warmer, and the little bit of dew that had fallen the night before was drying from the grass. The horses walked slowly side by side, and every now and then Gwen could feel Bo's eyes on her. She wondered if he was admiring the way she was managing the horse or laughing to himself. Gwen supposed if she did something that wasn't right he would tell her.

When they reached a gate at the west end of his property, Bo stepped down from Wings and opened it. Apple and Gwen passed through the gate. Bo proceeded through, leading Wings, and then closed the gate. "Beautiful mornin,' isn't it?

"Yes, it is, but I have a feeling that it's going to be very warm this afternoon." *I can't believe we're talking about the weather!* Once again they walked their horses in silence, and Gwen noticed it wasn't an uncomfortable silence but simply a silence shared by two friends. It was a good feeling.

Gwen also noticed the mountain that ran to the south of both of their ranches. She used to love that mountain, and she knew when spring was approaching because she could hear the whippoorwills calling in the trees announcing that poor chip had indeed fallen from a white oak. She always loved that sound. To her, it was a promise of another summer of lazy days lying in the sun, waking when she felt like it, and not having to watch for the school bus to come rumbling down the road. She looked at the mountain in a new light now. She saw many hardwood trees that might be turned into a cash crop if she ever needed money, and from what Bo had told her about feeding cows from October through April, she would probably need some money before she left the ranch next July. She would hate to liquidate all of this property in less than satisfactory condition. Her dad had made it work for all those years, and surely she could do the same, at least for one year.

"That didn't take long." Bo startled Gwen out of her private thoughts.

They had already reached the gate that led into Gwen's own pasture. Bo lightly stepped down, opened the gate, and let Gwen and Apple pass through. Pal and Roxie were right behind the horses, panting, grinning, and anticipating what was to come. *I wish I could muster that much enthusiasm.*

Suddenly Gwen remembered that the trip was not just a pleasure trip; they had work to do. A lump came up in her throat sort of like the one she would get in her throat when her mom would have to call the dentist for an appointment for her.

"Like I said, your dad didn't usually bring the cows out of the summer pasture until late September or early October; but there is no grass left up there, so you need to bring them in just in case you have to start feeding early. This grass here in the winter pasture looks pretty good, though. Maybe they can eat on this until November. When were you planning on taking your calves to market?"

"Bo, please." Gwen was exasperated. "Don't talk to me about things like that. You should know that you will have to tell me when to do those things. When do you take your calves to market?"

"Well, I usually watch the livestock market. When the market starts going up, I'll call and tell a hauler to come and get them in about a week and then hope that the market doesn't go down in that week. The market's crazy. I've seen the price of cows stay up all winter if we have a mild winter, but you can't second-guess the weather. If we have a sudden ice storm or a snowstorm, the market will drop, and that means dollars from your pocket. If you have enough money to last through the drop, you're okay. But if you are operating on a shoestring like most ranchers, you have to sell some of your cattle whether you want to or not. That's the only way you can feed what's left. Sometimes, if you're lucky, you may even have enough money left to buy a new pair of overalls."

"I was just thinking about money. I don't think my savings account will keep me going through the winter."

"What about the money that your dad left you?"

"What money?"

"I don't know. Your dad told me that he always had enough money put back from spring to see him through winter. I just thought that you had found out about that from his banker."

"No, I hadn't even heard about that until now. I'll do some calling and find out about it, though. I was thinking about checking to see if I could sell some of the timber off of the mountain to maybe raise money to buy feed for the cows."

"Don't cut that timber! That's some of the best deer woods in this country. This November, you will have to fight the hunters from the big cities off this mountain with a shotgun."

"Really?"

"Well, maybe I've exaggerated; but just a little bit. Everyone in these parts knows about your mountain, and they know that your dad didn't let anyone back in here to kill his deer. He deliberately left that mountain in timber just so the deer would have a place to hide during deer season." Bo was laughing now, and Gwen imagined that he was remembering some conversation that he and her father had had concerning the deer. Gwen found herself laughing at the thought of deer standing behind every tree, peeking out as the hunters drove down the county road not a quarter of a mile from them.

"If you need money to buy feed for the cows before spring, let me know. I have a little saved, and I would consider it a privilege to help winter Will's cows." Gwen didn't know why, but his comment hurt and irritated her just a little.

Before she knew it, and much before she was ready for it, they were at the big double gates that separated the summer and winter pastures. Gwen sat on Apple and stared at the wide expanse of land that lay before her. As far as she could see, the land was a crispy carpet of brown. There were very few trees, but what were there were turning autumn brown, and many leaves lay on the ground around the bases of the trees.

"Terrible, isn't it?" Bo remarked, noticing Gwen surveying the land.

"I was just thinking how strangely beautiful it is."

"Lady, this is not beautiful. It means that all of the ranchers in this area will have to start feeding early this year . . . and that means you too. We haven't had much rain for the past eighteen months. The ponds are drying up, and the pastures around here are all just like this one. No, this isn't beautiful."

"I'm sorry. I was just looking at the colors. I wasn't thinking of the drought." Gwen's voice was subdued, and she truly felt sorry for all of the ranchers in this area, including herself.

Bo sighed and turned to Gwen. "Oh well, we can't change the weather, and it's something that we all have to live with. Come on, let me show you this. You notice these gates? Let me show you how this works. Your dad was an amazing man."

Gwen didn't know whether or not to get down from Apple and wasn't certain if she did she would be able to get back on. "Do you want me to get down to see this?"

Bo turned, shaded his eyes against the east sun, and shook his head. "Naw, just keep your seat. I'll show you from where you are."

He proceeded to unlock the two twelve-foot gates and pulled one out toward her. The other he swung into the summer pasture. "Now when we go in and gather those cattle, they will naturally go to the fence line. All we have to do is keep them bunched next to the fence, and when we get them to the gates coming from the south, the north gate will turn them into the winter pasture. Neat, huh?"

Gwen was amazed at how simple he made it sound and also at the ingenuity of her father. She edged Apple through the open gates, and Bo, after remounting, followed.

He stood in his stirrups and scanned the land. "I don't see any cattle, but they're here somewhere. I just hope they're bunched and not scattered from here to Georgia. I'd like for your first experience at moving these cows to be an easy one. I don't think you're ready for any brush poppin'," he said, nodding his head toward the death grip Gwen still had on her saddle horn. Self-consciously, she loosened her grip and found that her left hand was stiff and achy. She stretched it until it felt flexible again.

Apple had given no problem, so Gwen laid her hand on her thigh. She had seen Bo do this, so she thought this was probably the proper way to ride.

They rode north along the fence and then west, topping a low rise. Apple suddenly threw her head up and pointed her ears forward. Gwen, once again gripping the saddle horn, looked ahead to where Apple was looking.

Below her stretched a wide expanse of dry, brittle grass. To her left she saw a small grove of trees; huddled beneath the trees was what appeared to be a lumpy patchwork quilt. Looking closer, she discerned cows, her cows. They were red with white faces, black with white faces, and a multitude of all colors in between. Gwen had had visions of a beautiful green pasture full of fat cows that looked like the pictures she had seen in an ice-cream store. These cows were anything but a picture.

Bo slowly turned Wings toward the cows. "If they break and run, you'd better have a good grip on that saddle. Apple will cow."

"She'll what?"

"She'll cow. It's natural in some horses. They act like they really enjoy chasing a cow. Just pull her back, and maybe you'll be okay."

Maybe? She tightened her hand around the saddle horn and felt her heart pounding

"You sit right here, and I'll see if I can get them to move over to the west fence. When you see them move toward the fence, just take Apple straight toward it in a slow walk. Easy does it." He smiled reassuringly.

He nudged Wings into a walk, making a wide circle around the cattle. The cattle were watching his every move, and a few of the mother cows could be heard softly lowing to their calves.

When the cattle began moving, Apple's ears sprang up, and Gwen could feel the mare's muscles tense. Gwen's heart was pounding in her throat and ears. She pulled back gently on the reins and spoke softly. "Easy, girl. Remember me? I'm the woman who knows absolutely nothing about this cow and horse thing." Gwen wanted to reach down and give her a pat on the neck as she had seen Bo do, but she was not about to release her bulldog grip on the saddle horn and wouldn't dare move the reins for fear that Apple would mistakenly think that Gwen wanted her to begin to "cow."

The herd began to move to the west fence, and Gwen gently moved Apple's reins. Apple responded as if she knew what to do. She slowly turned and walked toward the fence parallel to the cows. Turning to look at Bo, Gwen could see that he was gauging his distance cautiously for fear of spooking the cattle. If they began to speed up, he dropped back, and they would once again slow down. He turned to look at Gwen, threw her a smile, and held his hand up, making a circle with his index finger and thumb, indicating that everything was going well.

The cattle moved lazily south until they reached the fence and turned, heading east. Pal and Roxie were everywhere at once. They ran, nipping low at the heels of cows that lagged behind. When the cattle were moving well, the two border collies would lie down, panting hard but always on alert, waiting for a chance to do what they were bred and born for. All seemed to be going well, and Bo and Gwen talked as they rode.

When the southeast corner of the pasture was reached, the herd turned north.

"They act like they know where they're going," Gwen observed.

"They do. The older cows have done this same thing for years. They know there will be grass in the new pasture. Some of these cows have done this every year for ten or twelve years.

And, by the way, you need to think about clearing out some of the older cows. They can be sold, and with the money they bring, you can buy more feed for the rest. Also, you need to get rid of these steers. Just keep your momma cows."

"You're going to have to help me. I don't know how to tell old cows from young cows."

"That's why you need to find your father's books."

"Okay, I'll look this afternoon. Where are the bulls that you mentioned?"

"They're over at my place now. Your dad said I could use them. I'll bring them back if you need them."

"No thanks. You just keep them for as long as you need them. I don't like a bull any more than I like a stallion... No offense, Wings," Gwen added, looking at the sleek stallion walking beside Apple.

Soon Bo and Gwen reached the gate, and she could see how the opened gate turned the cattle into the winter pasture. Some of the cows saw the taller grass and began pushing faster through the gate. Calves were being pushed and butted out of the way. Suddenly a young heifer turned back into the pasture and ran from the herd. Gwen leaned forward, pointed, and shouted, "Bo, look!"

Apple, thinking Gwen was asking for action, sprang forward with a burst of lightning speed. Desperately, Gwen reached for the saddle horn, but the speed of the horse had her forced against the cantle of the saddle, and she only grabbed air.

It happened so quickly that Gwen wasn't aware of falling; but the next thing she knew, she was staring into clear blue sky, trying to retrieve the breath that had been forced from her by the impact of the fall.

She saw Bo leap from Wings's back and run toward her. He knelt beside her and cupped her head in his hand. "Are you hurt?" Concern showed on his face. Gwen tried to answer but nothing came out. "You've had the air knocked out of you. I'm sorry. I should have told you. When you lean forward in the saddle like that," he threw a thumb toward Apple, "she thinks you want her to take off." Gwen found her breath coming back.

"You're right on both counts." Gwen looked up at him.

He raised his brows in question. "Both counts?"

"Yes, you're sorry, and you should have told me."

"You can cut me down later. Right now I want to know if you hurt anywhere."

Gwen began a mental inventory of her respective parts. All of her respective parts answered by telling her that they were all somewhat hurt but nothing seemed to be broken.

"No, I don't think anything is broken, and only my pride seems to be hurting." She rose and began dusting

DONNA BARNARD

herself off. One ankle gave, and she drew her breath hard.

"Ouch, now that hurts but not too badly. I think I can make it."

"Here let me help you," Bo offered his hand, but Gwen held up a hand in refusal.

"No, thank you. I think I can manage by myself."

"Okay." Bo shrugged his shoulders and started walking toward Wings.

Gwen heard the sound of hoof beats. Looking past Bo, she saw Apple running the heifer that had escaped from the herd. The runaway made her way through the gate, and Apple came to a grinding halt.

"That's great," Gwen quipped as she limped toward Apple. "Next time I'll just send the horse, and I'll stay at home and have a glass of lemonade." Suddenly a wrenching pain shot through the calf of her right leg, and she was forced to sink back to the ground.

"You are hurt." Bo turned back to her. "Where?"

"My right leg." This time she was not so snappish with her answer. The pain made her head spin. She took a deep breath and raised her right knee to have a better look. The back of her pants leg was torn, and around the tear was a scarlet stain that was quickly growing.

Bo walked around behind her to have a better look. "You've probably hit a stob. Now will you let me help you?" He led Apple over to where Gwen was standing. He leaned over and laced his fingers, offering her a boost. Gwen placed her foot in his proffered hands and let him raise her to the saddle. "We need to get you to the house and have a look see at that. Sit tight while I shut these gates. First things first, you know."

First things first? I'm bleeding to death, and he closes a gate before attending to me! Bo returned and swept Apple's reins into his hands and mounted Wings. "Hold on, Dallas. You're gonna learn to ride a horse in a lope." He kicked the big horse into a lope, and surprising even herself, Gwen managed to stay on by gripping the horn with both hands. It wasn't long before Gwen felt a rhythm to the ride and let her body flow with it. The pain in her leg wasn't that bad, but because Bo acted as though there were something to be afraid of, Gwen felt fear. The trip back to the house seemed to take longer than the trip to the pasture, and Gwen was relieved to see her house come in sight.

When they arrived Bo carefully helped Gwen dismount and swept her into his powerful arms. She could feel the ripple of muscles in his arms and chest as he carried her into the relative coolness of the house. Just as she was being swept away in more ways than one, she was deposited unceremoniously on the ancient sofa. "Dallas, you need to take those pants off so I can take a look at your leg."

Gwen raised her eyebrows in mock surprise and modesty, but seeing the seriousness etched across his face, she lowered her eyes. "I'll go get a sheet so I can cover myself." She started to rise.

"Never mind. Stay where you are. I'll get one." Taking long strides, he disappeared toward the kitchen. Soon he returned with a rumpled sheet.

"Mission accomplished." She smiled, trying to lessen the grave expression on Bo's face.

Her attempt at levity was in vain because Bo bent, covered her with the sheet, and snapped, "Now, get those pants off. I'll go to the bathroom and see if I can find something to dress your leg." He turned and headed back toward the kitchen and down the hallway toward the bathroom.

She began struggling under the sheet to shed her pants. Bo returned and sighed with exasperation. Gwen slipped off her shoes and kicked them onto the floor. She managed to slip out of the khakis and slide them from her feet. Immediately, she saw the reason for his concern. The pants were blood soaked from knee to hem, and her foot and leg were encrusted with dried blood. She gasped when another pain shot through her leg.

"Lay back there and let me have a look."

She quietly submitted, let her head fall back on the sofa, and closed her eyes. The vision of her leg played through her mind, and she groaned. "What's the matter? I haven't even touched you yet." Bo snapped his head in her direction.

"Nothing," she muttered.

He gently cleaned the wound and the area around it, and Gwen was amazed at his gentleness. "That's not too bad. I guess you just bleed a lot." Gwen could hear the relief in Bo's voice.

She slowly opened her eyes and glanced at Bo. He was busy with an ointment and gauze. She closed her eyes again and could still see his profile. She saw the set of his jaw, the clean, sharp cheekbone, and the long auburn eyelashes. *I have to quit thinking about things like that.* She forced herself to see the little red sports car sitting in the show room ... clean, sharp lines. She quickly opened her eyes and made herself look at the faded curtains hanging over dusty windowpanes. She felt the bandage go on and Bo's fingers pressing the tape against her leg. He patted her leg just above the knee as he rose. "I have to go get those horses unsaddled."

She looked up to meet his eyes. "Thanks, Bo." She breathed a sigh of relief. "I'm sorry I'm such a mess."

"You're not a mess, Dallas." Bo smiled and turned for the door. "You're a challenge, and I love a challenge." He smiled. "I'll be back as soon as I take the horses over to the house and take care of them. You just stay right there and rest. I'll be back real soon. Don't be up on that thing," he said, indicating her leg. "I've got the bleeding stopped for now. If you get up, it'll probably start again. Just take it easy. Do you need anything before I go?"

"Yes, please. Would you mind handing me some water? There's a pitcher in the refrigerator."

He walked to the refrigerator, poured a glass of water, and brought it to her. After she had drunk, he asked if she need more. "No, thanks. I'll be fine; you go do what you need to do." Gwen hated to be any more trouble than she had already been.

"Okay." He headed out the door. "See ya soon." The screen door slapped shut behind him, and she heard him talking to Pal and the horses. He was still talking as she heard the sound of horses' hooves slowly move down the dusty road.

A tingle on her leg marked the place where seconds before Bo's hand had patted her. Quickly she took her hand and rubbed the spot gingerly. "This is ridiculous, Gwen," she admonished herself. "You can't have these feelings for him. He thinks you're the world's greatest klutz. He deserves a country girl who would know better than to lean forward on a horse that 'cows.'"

Wearily, Gwen laid her head back on the sofa and

DONNA BARNARD

closed her eyes. The heat was smothering, and she wondered why her mom and dad had never gotten air conditioning. The sweat was running from her stomach, sliding down her sides. "I'm going back to Dallas," she said to the hot air around her. "Back to an air-conditioned, seventh-floor apartment."

She dozed in a fitful sleep. Unsummoned, unbidden, something tugged at the rim of her thoughts. Vaguely, an indistinct figure walked the borders of her mind. She tried desperately to grasp the thought, to bring it in clearer, but as she crawled through the fog and approached the figure, it would elude her. She ran. It ran faster. She felt her legs being drawn from under her. She was falling. The figure turned toward her but there was no face. "Dallas," it called. "Dallas." *That's not my name. Why is it calling me that? That's not my name.* She snapped awake. She gasped.

CHAPTER FOUR

"Sorry, I didn't mean to scare you." Bo smiled and offered her a plate on which rested a sandwich. In his other hand was a glass of lemonade. "All I could find in the kitchen was peanut butter. I hope it's all right. You really need to buy some groceries."

Gwen pulled herself up to a sitting position. Her hair was wet and sticking to her face in ringlets. "I need air conditioning too. It's too hot." She reached for the lemonade and drank it down in one draught. She blew into the glass. The returning air was refreshing. She thought about removing the sheet that covered her legs but decided against it. "Thank you." She returned the glass to Bo's outstretched hand.

Bo placed the plate on her lap and returned to the kitchen to get more lemonade for Gwen and a large glass of water for himself.

"What about you?" Gwen asked through a bite of sandwich. "Aren't you going to eat?"

"I made me one too. I'll get it."

Gwen looked around the room. The mess that had covered the floor was gone and had been replaced by a small fan. The breeze, although warm, was refreshing. The two of them sat and munched slowly between talk about the price of cattle, and she listened intently. She knew that she would have to dip into the money she had been saving for the car to buy hay for the winter, but it still wouldn't be enough. Maybe she could sell enough cattle to feed the rest.

Bo sat patiently, answering all of her seemingly inane questions. After some time, Bo asked, "Dallas, I hate to poke my nose in, but are you broke? These questions you're asking seem to indicate a lack of funds." He took on the look of a benevolent loan officer as he rubbed his bewhiskered chin thoughtfully. Gwen knew that he was trying to make light of her serious situation.

"Well,"—she placed the empty plate on the coffee table—"I'm not broke. I have enough money to buy those groceries you mentioned, and I have enough to pay the electric bill if you turn the fan off… now. I have some savings, but since I don't know how much money I will need to see me through the winter, I don't know if I'll have enough."

Surprise on his face, Bo stood and picked up the plate and started to the kitchen. "You need to check at the bank. I know your dad wouldn't have left you with no money to run this place. He just wouldn't have done that."

"Okay, I'll call the bank. I know that Mom and Dad had about five hundred dollars in a savings account and a hundred or so in their checking, but I don't know if Dad had a separate account for the ranch. I'll check on that. I also need to call Dad's attorney. He said that he knew nothing about any more money that Dad had for the cows. I don't think I have enough to buy hay and feed and all those other things cows need," she said, pointing in the general direction of the pasture. *Will the car savings be enough to carry me through winter and spring?*

Bo settled back into his chair and thought for a moment. "Don't worry right now. You have the rest of the summer to let those cows pretty much take care of themselves now that they are where they belong. Pal, Roxie, and I went back up on the mountain and brought them down while you were napping."

He smacked both thighs with a resounding whack and rose, pushing his body up out of the chair. "I'm going to town," he announced. "I'll be back as quickly as I can. I suggest you rest; but you probably won't, so I'll just say take it easy. If your leg starts bleeding again, we may have a problem."

"Why are you going to town?" Gwen asked and then realized it was really none of her business. "Sorry, I didn't mean to pry."

"I'll be back," he said, evading her question. In a second he was out the door. Gwen heard him speaking to Pal as he went. She heard the truck door open, close, and the engine fire. She listened as long as she could and was shocked to realize that she hated to see Bo leave. The quietness and solitude of the house, the situation with the cows, and the lack of money all seemed to fall in on her. A tear slid down her cheek to the corner of her mouth. The salty taste startled her. "You idiot! Get your mind off your situation. You can't do anything about it right now anyway." She shook her head. "I'm just feeling sad because I don't know what to do and I have no money. That's it. I'm just feeling sorry for myself." She pushed up from her reclining position to find she was slightly light-headed, and she ached in every stiff joint of her body. She sank back on the sofa and breathed heavily. "This isn't going to be easy, is it?" Slowly she pulled herself into a sitting position. She sat rigidly for a moment then swiveled her body so she could lower her feet to the floor. The injured leg throbbed, and a streak of pain went through her right hip. "Gwen," she spoke softly to herself, "you are an idiot. Get up from here and do something." She eased herself from the sofa. "Oh." She groaned. "I know what something I'm going to do. I am going to take a hot bath and see if I can soak some of this misery from my bones."

She lurched her way to the bathroom and started running water into the tub. She passed the mirror and turned in horror. Her hair was stringing down in moist tendrils, and sticking out in every direction were pieces of dried grass. Her face was dirty, and there were circles under each of her dark brown eyes. Her cheeks were sunburned to a deep red, as were her upper arms and shoulders. Where tears had streamed down her face there was what appeared to be mud. She grinned, laughed, then winced from the pain. "It only hurts when I laugh, Doc," she said jokingly into the mirror. She leaned in closer. "He has never seen you in anything but a mess." She put on her most seductive look, raised one eyebrow, and in a breathy tone with as much of a French flavor as an Oklahoma accent would allow, told the dirty face in the mirror, "Just, vait you *vill* be yourself again." She removed the remainder of her clothing and stepped into the bathtub with her good leg. A slight moan escaped her lips as she lowered her body into the water. Slowly she lifted the injured leg onto the side of the tub. She gasped. The pain was pretty bad, but it was just going to have to wait. She sank into the warm water. It was heavenly, but she wanted to be ready when Bo returned, so she grudgingly sat up and started scrubbing at the day's dirt. Grime gave way to squeaky clean, and she felt refreshed ... body and soul.

After a bath and shampoo, she stood—still wet with one towel wrapped around her head and another around her body—and studied her features closely. "Hmm, not too bad, I guess."

As she was making her way into the bedroom, she looked down and saw that her leg had indeed begun bleeding again. She knew it would have to be redressed, and she also knew that she would have to do it herself. She returned to the bathroom and reached into the medicine cabinet to retrieve the dressing, antibiotic ointment, and tape. Gwen didn't want Bo to think she was totally helpless, so she steeled herself, sat down on the top of the stool, and removed the bandages. *I can do this. I can change this bandage.* A wry grin crossed her face. At work she was the epitome of self-confidence but so far, since she had been back at her childhood home, she was like a little, defenseless kid. She wrinkled her nose, closed her eyes, and pulled the bandage off and peeked from one eye. The wound was still bleeding, so she pressed hard with a towel until it stopped. She rushed to finish the job. Not only because time was of the essence but also because she didn't want to look at the leg any more than she had to.

After dressing the wound, she quickly got herself

DONNA BARNARD

dressed in shorts, T-shirt, and canvas sneakers. She limped back into the bathroom and realized that her next problem was her still-wet hair. Analyzing the problem, she decided the safe thing to do was to brush it into a ponytail and let it go at that. Of course, she would try to make it the perkiest ponytail possible. As she was brushing her hair into place, she thought, *What am I doing? Am I leading Bo on? I don't usually like that one-night-stand thing.* "Well," she announced to the mirror, "I'm going to be here for another eleven months. That's not a one-night stand." *I am not going to stay in this place any longer than I have to, though. I don't like it here. I never liked it here. I like cocktail parties. I like drinks with the crew after work ... I love that little red sports car, and that's on my list for the first thing I'll buy when I sell this place. I like my apartment. I like ... well, I like everything about my work and Dallas and ... oh, well. Someday, I will be happy again.*

She added a little more color to her sunburned cheeks and drew lipstick across her windburned, sunburned lips. The effect was clownish. She gave a disgusted look at the mirrored image, stuck her tongue out, crossed her eyes at it, and lathered up a washcloth. She scrubbed until what makeup was there was gone and her nose and cheeks shined. She dabbed on some moisturizer and rubbed it in well. What she saw pleased her. The pallor that she had tried to disguise behind unimaginable dollars worth of makeup while living in Dallas was gone. The person who stared back at her from the mirror looked healthy and vibrant. She smiled. Suddenly, she realized something. She was relatively happy! She didn't have a job; she didn't know if she had enough money to live for the next year; she had two hundred creatures depending on her as their sole source of provision, and she was happy. "You must be crazy," she whispered to herself. "You have to be stark-raving crazy. And you're not going to lead that man on any more. You may be here for only a year, but during that time, you and he will just have to settle for being friends. You can be perfectly happy having Bo as a friend. No leading him on." She wagged her finger at herself, chidingly.

She gimped her way back into the living room and decided that she had better straighten up a bit before she rested. She picked up the sheet, wadded it up, and took it to place on the washer. The lid was up. She peered inside, and there soaking in cold water were her torn, bloody pants. *Hmmm, he's so nice,* she thought. *He's smart too. He even knows how to pre-treat stained clothing.* She chuckled to herself. "You sound like a television commercial." She laughed and threw the sheet into the hamper, poured herself another glass of water on her way through the kitchen, and returned to the living room to sit in front of the fan and wait for Bo.

Her wait wasn't long. She saw Pal rise from where he was sleeping on the porch. He knew the sound of Bo's truck. His stubby tail began wagging. She couldn't hear Bo's truck; but she knew that Pal could and that was good enough for her. She patted her hair, sat up a little straighter, and placed her feet on the coffee table. The move caused another pain in her hip but alleviated the throbbing in her leg.

Her heart jumped a little when she heard the sound of Bo's truck door slam. *Stop being silly, Gwen,* she scolded herself. *You're acting like a junior-high girl. What do you want with a cowboy anyway? Get your priorities straight. You love your job. You love Dallas. You can be happy here for a year, and when your year here is over, you'll return to Dallas.* She took a deep breath and looked toward the front porch. Through the screen she could see him.

"Dallas, you awake?"

"Sure, come on in, Bo!" she shouted to the screen.

Bo walked in and stood for a moment, letting his eyes adjust to the sudden dimness of the house. In his arms were brown paper bags sporting a cardinal, the insignia of the town's grocer.

"Hey, you look a little better." He grinned. "At least, you look cleaner." His eyes playing approvingly over her body made Gwen blush. She hadn't blushed since she was in the third grade and Robert Baumgartner had kissed her.

He walked into the kitchen and shouted back to Gwen. "I'm gonna fix something for us to eat. I figured since you're lame I'd pitch in and do some cooking. It's the only time, you understand. I don't like to show off my culinary talents as a chef very often."

"Now, that's nice of you," Gwen said, straightening her pillow on the sofa. "What are we having—bologna sandwiches?"

Bo stuck his head through the kitchen door with an exaggerated look of hurt pride and disappointment on his face. "Madam, we are having an epicurean's delight. Southern fried catfish, hushpuppies, pan-fried potatoes, and for dessert … ta da … lemon meringue pie."

Gwen was amazed. Realizing that her bottom jaw had dropped, she closed her mouth and added, "I'm impressed. I really am. I didn't know you were so versatile."

"Dallas, there's myriad things that you don't know about me."

Gwen was taken aback. He was right. She knew very little about this man, but she knew that if her father liked him and allowed him to sit on the porch and visit that she was probably safe. After all, this wasn't Dallas. This was Long Prairie, Oklahoma. She started to rise. "Do you want me to help? I feel much better."

"No." He held his hands up and rushed over to the sofa. "No, you stay put. I want to do it all by myself. Please. I want to do it for you."

He gently but firmly urged her back to the sofa. "Just relax."

He turned quickly and blew back into the kitchen.

Pots and pans began to clatter, and occasionally Gwen could hear a *"dadgumit"* or a *"shoot"* spat out in frustration. Soon delicious smells began to find their way into the living room to remind her that a peanut-butter sandwich wasn't much food for an entire day. Gwen's stomach began to growl, and her mouth watered.

While she was waiting for dinner to be prepared, she let her mind wander back to her days in Dallas, her job, and her friends. She had several friends, but all were in some way connected with her work. She had found herself in Dallas as a young girl, and she needed friends. The job that she found held a wealth of them. *I wonder how my friends would like Bo. I wonder how Bo would like my friends.* Bo, she supposed, could get along with anyone. Slowly a plan began to form in her mind. *I can't go to Dallas because of the responsibilities of the ranch, but there's no reason why my friends can't come to the ranch for a holiday. They might even enjoy getting out*

DONNA BARNARD

of Dallas for a few days. T.J., Lance, and Kaycee would come for sure. That should do it. She didn't think that the little two-bedroom house was large enough for any more than that. She would invite them up over the Thanksgiving holidays. It would be fun—sitting around the fireplace, talking. *Oh, no fireplace. Okay, sitting around the wood stove.* Yes, it would be fun.

"Are you ready to eat?" Bo interrupted her thoughts. "It's about ready. Do you want to eat in here? The kitchen is a mess, and I think that you should have that leg elevated anyhow." After answering his own question, he turned and disappeared into the kitchen again.

Maybe Bo could help with the Thanksgiving meal, she thought. That would involve him in the fun. *I want them to meet him. He's such a dear.* She shocked herself by using one of T.J.'s favorite expressions. Bo wasn't "a dear." He was a nice guy, but to T. J., everyone was a dear.

Gwen's coworkers would be shocked to find she had a friend here—a cowboy friend. *The guys at work aren't really snobs. Beneath that stuff-shirt exterior are hearts of gold.* "I hope so anyway," she said aloud.

Bo walked out of the kitchen. "Huh?"

"What?" Gwen was shocked to know she had said the last words aloud.

"Oh, I was just thinking out loud. Wow! Look at you."

Bo was making his way back into the living room, performing a balancing act with her supper.

"Sorry, but I couldn't find a TV tray."

Gwen chuckled. "Why would Mom and Dad have a TV tray when they didn't even have a TV? Dad always said, 'Televisions make softies of mankind.' My parents didn't have air conditioning or any heat other than that woodstove." She threw a hand toward the stove sitting in the corner. "They didn't even have indoor plumbing until I was in junior high."

Bo smiled and got a faraway look in his eyes. "I know."

"Don't tell me, let me guess, you don't have a television either?"

Bo bent down to put her supper tray on her lap. He had used one of her mom's cookie sheets for a lap tray.

"I didn't say that. I said your dad told me that. Most of his advice was good, and I followed it; but I didn't listen to that. I have a TV, but I rarely have time to watch it." Gwen looked down at the tray sitting across her lap and felt her mouth begin to water. "This looks wonderful! I didn't realize how hungry I am."

"I'll go get my plate and join you in here."

As her eyes studied the plate before her, she thought, *Yes, he can definitely help with the meal.* Before her lay a beautifully browned catfish fillet and all the trimmings.

The aroma made her stomach protest loudly at having to wait.

"I heard that." He put his plate on the coffee table. "Go ahead," said Bo. "Don't wait on me. After all, this is your house." Bo brought a chair from the kitchen and sat down opposite her and watched as she popped the first bite into her mouth.

It was delicious. She closed her eyes and savored the taste. "Oh, Bo, this is wonderful."

Gwen could have sworn she heard him release a breath. Apparently he had been worried that she wouldn't like what he had prepared. He smiled broadly, and his ruddy face beamed with pride.

She was shocked to see him fold his hands and lower his head. She immediately followed suit. "Thank you, Lord, for not letting Dallas get seriously hurt today. And we thank you, Lord, for this food. Amen."

Gwen added, "And thank you for the one who prepared this meal," and echoed his amen and sat for a second and looked at this enigma that was Bo Bohanan. His face reddened. Gwen felt the muscles of her throat tighten, and her intake of breath was almost a gasp. *Just keep remembering the apartment that you are still paying a lease on and that little red sports car.*

"Too hot?"

"N-No," she stammered. "It's just right. Where did you learn to cook like this? This is wonderful!"

"When one"—he pointed to himself—"has something to do, why not do it to the best of your ability? Well, actually, when I was a kid, I had asthma, so I had to stay in the house a lot. I learned to cook with my mom. She taught me well."

She nodded in agreement, and returned to her feast. When they finished, Bo removed the plates from her tray, went to the kitchen, and returned with pie and coffee.

"The pie is store bought." He said, apologizing. "I'm not too good at pies."

The pie and coffee complemented the meal, and as they both ate the last crumbs, Gwen decided to ask Bo about Thanksgiving dinner. "Bo, how would you like to help me with Thanksgiving dinner?"

He gave her a puzzled look. "What do you mean?"

"I'm going to invite some of my friends up from

Dallas, and I would like it if you would help me fix dinner for them."

A hurt look crossed his face. "You mean you want me to cater your little affair?" Gwen could see that he was hurt by her suggestion.

"Not at all. I want you to come to dinner also. I want us, you and me, to fix dinner together. I just need a little help. In case you hadn't noticed, I'm not much of a cook. If you and I worked together, I might actually learn something."

"Together?" He raised his eyebrows. Rubbing his chin, he said, "Let me see, you want me to help you prepare the dinner, and then I get to stay and eat too? I get to eat with your friends?"

"Yes," she answered, puzzled.

"May I eat in the dining room with them, or do I have to eat in the kitchen?"

"Bo, are you teasing or are you really angry?"

The stern look stayed on his face. "I'm only teasing," he answered and threw Gwen one of those breathtaking smiles. "You don't have a dining room, remember?"

"Yes, I do happen to remember that. I just don't want to spend the holidays alone. With the folks gone ... you know. And I was hoping that we could spend the holidays together. That is, unless you have other plans. Do you have family coming in, or had you planned on going somewhere?"

"No, none of the above," he answered. "Neither of us is going to spend the holidays alone. You and I will prepare a repast fit for kings and queens."

"We will?"

"Yeah," he rose, took her coffee cup from her, and started toward the kitchen. "I figured I might teach you to operate a chain saw, but I guess I could teach you how to cook. That might also come in handy someday." He turned back to her, smiled, and winked. A lump came up in her throat, and she was having trouble getting her breath. She closed her eyes. *Remember the red sports car... the red sports car... the red sports car.*

Bo returned to the kitchen and apparently started cleaning up from the sounds that Gwen was hearing. The air was beginning to cool as evening approached.

Bo stuck his head through the kitchen door. "Hey, how about I make us some tea, and we go out on the back porch and watch the sun go down?"

"Sure, I'll come help."

"No, you won't. You need to rest that leg. I can see that you've already had to redress it. You go ahead to the porch, and I'll bring the tea."

Gwen rose and slowly made her way through the back screen. As soon as Pal heard the door shut, he came grinning and wagging to the back porch. "Hey, boy, where have you been?" Pal edged up to her and, resting his head on her knee, looked up with pleading eyes. A scratch behind his ears brought a look of sheer ecstasy.

Bo came backing through the door carrying two glasses of iced tea. His smile bounced from Gwen to Pal. "Here you go." He held both glasses out to her. "If you'll hold these, I'll pull up a chair for your leg."

He pulled a lawn chair over to the swing. She raised her leg to the seat and found that resting her leg did make it feel better.

Bo eased down into the swing and took a long drink of tea. Pal retreated to the nearest shade and sprawled out, belly down with all four legs spread out.

As the evening cooled and dusk set in, the two sat, comfortable in their silence. The only sound in the deepening darkness was the clink of ice in their glasses and the whippoorwills calling to one another.

Bo rose, held out his hand for her glass. "More?"

"Yes, please."

Shortly her tea glass was returned, filled.

Stars became visible in the night sky. "Nice evening, huh?" Bo observed.

"Um-hum. Nice. Bo, do you mind if I ask how you wound up here in Long Prairie?"

"Not at all. I was born and reared in a small town in California; the only child of two doctors. My father was killed in an automobile accident when I was nine years old.

"As a kid I always wanted to be a cowboy. I loved John Wayne movies and would imagine what it would be like to ride a horse and go on a cattle drive, but life has a way of changing our priorities. My mom died when I was a senior in high school, and since she always wanted me to be a doctor or a lawyer, as soon as I graduated, I sold the house and used the little bit of insurance money and the money from the sale of the house to go to law school."

"You're a lawyer?" Gwen asked incredulously.

"Yes, I am an attorney, but please don't hold that against me. After college, I got a job with a very good law firm in Los Angeles. I was doing very well, and I was satisfied but not truly happy. I was sitting, reading the paper one evening and there was a story about a sixty-five-car pile-up out on Highway 101. Several people were killed. I just started thinking about those people who had lost their lives that day. They had dreams. They had plans. I imagine they were planning a cookout for the coming weekend. They were thinking about buying a new car or trying to decide what color to paint the kitchen. They never got to complete their plans and maybe not even a final thought. I made up my mind that day that if God ever gave me an opportunity to realize my dreams, I was going to take it. I began checking with several real estate agencies for an established ranch. I found the Janway place, which was being sold lock, stock, and barrel. It was perfect. Everything I needed to start living my dream except the knowledge to do it. That's where your dad came in ... You look like him, you know," Bo said offhandedly.

"I do?"

"Yes, you do. Same color hair ... same brown eyes, same smile ... ," he said softly, smiling at her. "Anyway, like I was saying, I would have given up in the first month, but your dad took pity and helped me learn the ropes, so to speak. It's been six years now, and I wouldn't trade it for anything."

"And now you're returning the favor?"

"I hope I am. Well,"—he slapped his thighs and rose—"I gotta go. Do you need help doing anything before I go?"

"No, not really, but I do have another question. If you've lived here for six years, then you knew my mom, right?"

"Yes, I knew her. She didn't have too much to say about running a ranch, but she made sure I had a home-cooked meal at least once a week; and her biscuits, m-m-m light as a feather!"

"Yep, that would be Mom. Always doing for someone else."

Slowly Gwen rose, testing her leg. "Thanks for everything. I appreciate it."

He reached for her empty glass. "Let me take these in the kitchen and you get some rest. G'night. I'll see you tomorrow."

DONNA BARNARD

CHAPTER FIVE

The next morning, Gwen woke with a smile on her face. The previous night she had gotten to know Bo a little better and she felt good about that. He was open and had talked more than she had ever heard him talk since she had met him.

For mid-August, the morning breeze was cool and refreshing as it found its way across her bed. Slowly she stretched. The injury on her leg brought her up short but felt better than yesterday—just felt a little stiff.

There was something different about this morning. There was a new smell on the breeze. It was familiar but also strange. She lay back on the cool sheets. Suddenly, she remembered. It was rain. Her mom and dad could smell rain, and now, apparently, so could she. Rain would please Bo. He had said the ranchers needed rain badly. She smiled. She was talking about some anonymous people out there in the world and realized that she, too, was one of those people who needed rain. "I'm a *rancher*," she said to the ceiling. That didn't sound too bad, so she tried it again after clearing her throat. "*I am a rancher.*" She enunciated each syllable. "Nope, not too bad at all."

Gwen decided that if it was going to rain she would continue cleaning house and doing laundry. She threw her legs over the side of the bed and slowly rose. She tested the injury. It was stiff and a little painful but not too bad.

She made her way into the laundry room and snapped on the washer. The pants were still in there from yesterday, so after adding detergent, she went to the kitchen to make coffee. Far to the south she heard the portentous growl of thunder. Because she had always loved that sound, she stopped and listened, smiling to herself. Walking to the back door of the house and looking out to the south, toward the mountain, she could see ominous clouds gathering. The wind was getting up, and she took a deep breath and held it. The thunder rolled again. *Maybe I should clean cabinets and closets today.* The aroma of coffee found its way out the back door too. She walked back to the kitchen, poured herself a cup, and returned to the porch. Gwen decided to just sit for a while and watch the storm approach. For the first time since she had been back in Oklahoma, it was not stifling; the breeze off the oncoming rain was cool. Sipping her coffee, she thought, *I feel like something good is going to happen. I am going to accomplish a lot today. I need to, anyway. A good cleaning will work wonders. I'll clean Mom and Dad's room.* She clicked off things from a mental list. *I need to call T. J. and invite everyone up before they make plans for Thanksgiving.* It was still three months away, but if you were going to make plans with T.J., you had to make them well in advance.

Walking back into the house, she heard the phone ring. It was Bo. He had decided that since it was raining and he couldn't do anything outside, he was going to be doing some work in the inside. Gwen laughed and told him of her plans, and they agreed that they would talk that evening.

After refilling her cup, she walked out the back door, sat down in the porch swing, and began swinging back and forth, drinking her coffee. Just as the last drop of coffee was drained, the first loud plops of rain could be heard hitting the roof. It didn't take long for the rain and the wind to send her rushing to the door. "Oh well, it's time to go to work anyway." A flash of lightning cracked across the sky, and thunder reverberated through the floor and tickled her feet, which made her think of her leg. Her leg felt much better this morning and after she redressed it, it felt more like a bruise. She decided she could work with that. The rain fell throughout the day, and by dusk she had all of the housework done except for her parents' room. She had put it off until last. She could barely bring herself to go into the room. Deciding to put it off a little longer, she reached for the phone. It was dead, but she guessed that was a good thing. She reminded herself of Mr. Foster who had died a few years back while talking on the phone during a thunderstorm. Lightning had struck the phone line. After that her dad wouldn't allow anyone to talk on the phone if there was the slightest chance of a storm coming. She turned back to her house cleaning.

She sighed deeply with resignation, walked to her

parents' room, and pushed the door open. She stood in the gathering gloom looking into the bedroom. A flash of lightning illuminated the space momentarily and showed her mom's hand-crocheted bedspread. The room was damp and musty. She had closed it the day she arrived for her father's funeral and hadn't opened it since.

"This is silly, Gwen. The house is yours now. This bedroom is yours too. There are no ghosts here. Go in there and get to work. The room has to be cleaned because you're going to have company … maybe."

She laughed at herself, reached into the room, and switched on the light.

Talking to the room, she asked, "Okay, where do I start?" She looked all around, and as if she heard an answer, turned to retrieve the cardboard boxes, which she had left in the hallway.

She dropped the boxes in front of the closet, sighed, opened the door wide, and began taking everything out of the closet, going through each piece. If it was relatively good, it went into a box for the church. The rest of the things would be trashed. The rain had slackened somewhat, and the silence of the house was deafening. Gwen turned on the ancient radio and listened to the popping, cracking music, which was interrupted by the many weather bulletins. Several counties were under a tornado watch; but Gwen wasn't afraid of tornados, and none of the counties mentioned were close by.

The work went quickly from the closet, to the dresser, to the chest of drawers, and finally to her mom's cedar chest. The chest had been a wedding gift from her dad. Only her mom's most precious belongings went into the chest; her mom called it Precious

DONNA BARNARD

Memories. Gwen hesitated for a moment, feeling as though she was intruding or prowling into her parents' things. Kneeling before the chest and slowly pushing the lid open, she smiled. Greeting her was a toothless, drooling grin. It was one of her baby pictures. Many baby pictures were scattered across the top of the contents, as if someone had been looking through them. She began lifting things from the chest. Many things were strange to her. She had no idea why her mom had kept some of them.

Some of the things were torn, discolored, and rotting. These she placed in a box that she planned on discarding. *There's no need in being sentimental about things that mean nothing to me.* In the bottom of the cedar chest lay a cardboard box whose top was somewhat caved in from the weight of the other items. She lifted it out and popped the lid open. It was full of papers, pictures, letters, and cards. There was her mom and dad's marriage license and a greeting card signed by some unknown person. There was Gwen's third grade report card and a copy of the one and only family picture that her mom could ever talk her dad into. Gwen was sitting on her mom's lap with a goofy jack-o-lantern grin on her face, Mom was grinning from ear to ear, and Dad was his usual somber self. There was a Bible, which had been given to Gwen's mom when *her* mother, Grandma Brownlee, died. The Bible had belonged to Grandma Brownlee and was the only thing that Gwen's mom, now she, had that had belonged to her grandmother. Tears welled and spilled down Gwen's face as she remembered the fun times that she, Grandma, and her mom had just going on a picnic. Her mom's smiling face floated into her mind, as did the bittersweet memory of the sadness that flitted across her face when Gwen's dad would insist that her picnics were a waste of time. He always had something else to do and would never go on one of the many picnics that the three ladies had gone on. Grandma would laugh and say, "Three generations of Brownlee girls on a Sunday picnic." Her grandmother's voice echoed in Gwen's head.

A flash of light brought Gwen out of her reverie. "This is no time to be thinking of a picnic. That's for sure." The rain once again pounded a rhythm on the roof, and the wind suddenly became stronger.

Gwen lifted the Bible out of the box, and an envelope slipped from the Bible to the floor. She picked it up, and on the envelope, written in her mom's large, rounded handwriting, was her name. Gwen sat and stared at the yellowed envelope, afraid to open it and afraid not to. Her fingers lingered over the flap for a moment more and then, with a ragged sigh, she lifted it and withdrew the letter.

May 17, 1967
My darling Gwen,
Today you graduated from high school. I am so proud of you. You are the light of my life. You are the only child that God saw fit to give me, so I figured I had been given the very best. I always thought your father would have preferred a son to help on the ranch, and because of my own feelings on that matter, I have alienated you from your father. I have always tried to keep you to myself for fear that you would see the disappointment in your father's eyes.
I was so wrong. Your father loves you so very much. He is very proud of you as a daughter and as a person.

I am so sorry for what I have done to him and to you. The two of you have lost years of love and happiness that could have been shared. I suppose if you are reading this, I am gone. Please, please help your father through this. You are all he has now. You have to be strong for him.

This ranch means everything to us, Gwen. I know I have turned you against ranch life because I wanted more for you, but your dad and I have put our whole lives into this ground, not for ourselves, but for you and for all the generations that spring from us. I hope that all of our work has not been in vain. I hope that there is enough of your father in you for you to realize that this land is what we have lived for all these years. When all of this land is gone, what will we have? God's not making any more of it, except maybe for Hawaii, I've heard. Ha ha.

Don't cry for me. I have enjoyed every minute on this earth and on this land. I only hope God has a place in the country for me. Gwen, if you ever need help, turn in God's Word to Hebrews 11:15.

I pray for you, your success, and your happiness every day. I love you, sweetheart. Don't give up. Be patient, and Dad can help you love the land as much as he does.

Love,
Mom

Gwen could hardly read the last of the letter for the tears. She wiped them on a baby blanket that had been wrapped in tissue paper in the cedar chest. She supposed it wasn't the first time that the blanket had soaked up her tears. She touched the letter to her cheek in an attempt to be closer to the paper, a piece of paper that her mother had touched. She wept long and hard for a mother who had loved her so, and for her father who also loved her; but until now, Gwen never realized how much. They were both gone now. She had lost both of them and couldn't tell them that she loved them too. She wept, rocking back and forth while she held the letter next to her chest, next to her heart. She lay back on the floor, pulled her knees up toward her chin, and cried.

When lightning knocked out the electricity, she did not stir. She lay in the darkness of her parents' bedroom floor. *I guess Dad was supposed to give this to me when Mom died. He may not have known it was here.* The wind, rain, thunder, and lightning sang her a lullaby. She fell into a deep sleep on the floor, cradling the letter from her mother with her baby blanket thrown over her shoulders. The letter had been delivered three years too late. She could never do anything about that, and for this she was truly sorry. She was sorry for her father, her mother, and for herself.

DONNA BARNARD

CHAPTER FIVE

Morning found Gwen curled into a tight ball, clutching the letter, the baby blanket, and feeling as if she had a balled-up sock in her mouth. She could hardly see through her swollen eyes.

She pulled herself into a sitting position and looked around. Her mind was fuzzy, and she had to think for a minute to remember why she was here in her parents' bedroom. Remembering, she looked down at the letter she held tightly in her fist and raised it to her nose, breathing deeply. It smelled like the inside of the cedar chest. Carefully folding it, she placed it back in the yellowed envelope and slowly picked up all of the things that she had removed from the chest the night before and replaced them. She looked down at her hands and noticed that they were dirty from the accumulated dust in the room. What she needed was a shower. She rose to a standing position. Although the pain in her leg brought her up short, it was much better than yesterday. Removing her clothes and dropping them to the floor, she walked to the bathroom. She decided that the shower could wait until she had made coffee, so she pulled on a robe and made her way to the kitchen.

She thought she would try to find the farm books that Bo had mentioned while the coffee was making. *I hadn't even thought of him this morning. I wonder if the phone is still not working.* She picked up the receiver and listened—silence. She went back into her parents' bedroom and, remembering her dad getting some books from a metal box that sat on the top shelf of the closet, she opened the closet door and looked above where the her parents' clothes had been hanging. The box was there. She reached up high and pulled it down. Inside were journals from years back. Finding a book, which had last year's date on it, Gwen opened it. The lettering was in her dad's precise printing, and numbers were all over the page; but she might as well have been looking at hieroglyphics. Carrying the book to the kitchen, she laid it on the table and poured a cup of coffee.

Bo will be glad that I found the ranch books. Tears welled in her eyes when she thought of Bo. *No, it's not Bo. It's the remainder of last night. I miss Mom so much. Thoughts of Bo should make me feel better.* She checked the phone again, just in case.

Things don't change around here much. The phone always goes out when we have a hard rain. She replaced the receiver and walked back into the bedroom to finish her work.

She hadn't gotten to the end of the hallway when the phone rang. Startled, she turned and went back into the kitchen. "Hello?"

"Good morning," Bo said, a smile in his words.

"Well, good morning yourself." And suddenly Gwen felt it *was* going to be a good morning. "I thought the phone was out."

"Oh, you just have to understand the phones around here. When it rains, they go out. It's just that simple. When the water runs down a bit, they come back on. I sure do appreciate that rain. It was just what we needed…even if the phones were out. What are you doing?"

"I just brought one of Dad's farm books in the kitchen for you to look at. I just don't understand what it all means, so I'll just wait 'til you come over to help me with it."

"I have to do chores, but I'll be over there as soon as I can. Do you have a pot of coffee made?"

Gwen laughed. "Yes, I do."

"Okay. Give me a while, and I will be over."

Gwen rushed back into the bathroom to take a quick shower. She let the cool water run over her face. *I hope this takes some of the swelling out of my eyes.* Quickly she dried off, pulled her hair into a ponytail, brushed her teeth, and applied moisturizer to her face. Removing the wet bandage from her leg, she noticed that it was much better this morning. Instead of redressing it with gauze bandage, she dried the area carefully and applied a large Band-aid. She pulled on shorts and a T-shirt then went back to the kitchen and decided she probably needed to make more coffee. After filling her cup once more, she poured the remainder in a thermos, and made another pot.

She sat down at the table, took a sip of hot coffee, and started absently flipping through the farm book and found an envelope tucked in between two pages. Lifting the envelope, she peered inside. Her eyes opened wide in surprise, and her mouth fell open. She couldn't believe it! It was a Certificate of Deposit made out in her name in the amount of five thousand dollars. Suddenly she thought of her dad. The CD was purchased three years ago—right after her mom died. *Dad knew this would happen. He wanted us to do this together. He wanted to be a part of my transition.* Thank you, Dad," she said as she hugged the envelope to her chest. "Thank you, thank you, thank you." She turned her eyes to the picture of Christ above the piano, "And thank you, Sir."

Gwen heard a knock at the door. "Come on in!"

"Howdy." Bo smiled as he came into the kitchen. "Are you prepared for a day of lessons in money management on the ranch?"

"I don't know if I'm up to it, but I'm ready." As she returned his smile, she could see that Bo noticed the swelling of her eyes and was thankful that he didn't mention it. Today she felt that she had something to smile about. The dread of a hard winter with no money was at least partially relieved.

Bo poured himself a cup of coffee and parked his long frame at the table. He tossed the CD off the book. She sipped and listened to his "uh huh … hummm" for about fifteen minutes. Bo would frown, and Gwen would feel her brow knit. He would smile, and her face would break out in a smile. A look of puzzlement would be evident on his face, and she hoped that he would not turn to her for an answer.

He raised his head and smiled. "I see what your father has done here, and if you're ready for your lesson to begin, I think I can explain it all to you just as soon as you pour me another cup of that coffee."

"Okay." She rose and filled his cup. "I guess I'm not too good at being a hostess this morning. I've been really excited." At the thought of the CD, a prickle of doubt flashed through her mind. *Should I show him? Of course, I should. I'm just being silly.* She reached over, picked up the envelope, and handed it over to Bo. "I found this in the book. Is it enough to last me for a while?"

Bo opened the envelope, pulled the CD out, and looked at it for a moment. "How 'bout that? Ol' Will did leave you something, didn't he? I was just sure he had, but I kind of figured it would be more than this." He waved the CD back and forth, fanning himself.

She poured herself another cup of coffee from the thermos. "Well, what do you think? Do I have enough to last for a while?"

"Well, I suppose this will just about pay for enough hay to see you through the winter. You'll also have the money from the sale of the cattle. Out of that..." He trailed off, writing figures on a sheet of paper.

"Well, let's just have a look-see. Look here. This is what Will spent on cattle at this time last year. We'll just have to go from here."

Over the next few hours, Bo patiently explained the ins and outs of how much was required to care for a ranch the size of Gwen's inheritance, and she began to wonder if she had enough money to last through the day.

"I don't have any money at all, do I? Not compared to what I'll need."

"Now wait a minute. The money that you have to

spend to sell your cattle is just invested money. How else are you going to get those cows to market? You're going to have to have help in doing that, and then you will be happier than ever when you see that money start to come in. I checked on the price of cattle this morning, and I think now is the time to sell. I'll call some folks, if you want yours sold at the same time I sell mine. We may even get a good deal since we're neighbors. The trucks won't have so far to go to get the second batch. What do you say? Do you want me to see if I can round up some hands and line out some trucks to help out?"

Things seemed to be going too fast for Gwen. Bo was waiting for an answer, the one thing she didn't want him to need right now. She looked into those liquid blue eyes and saw herself reflected in them. She thought only a second more before she agreed to let him take over.

He picked the CD up from the table. "First thing you need to do is to go to the bank and deposit this thing. You need to be prepared to pay the cowboys and truckers on the day the cows are picked up. Okay?" He raised his eyebrows, waiting for her answer.

"Okay."

Bo rose and walked to the door. "Hey, do you want to come over to my house for supper tonight? I haven't been very neighborly, have I?" He smiled and rubbed his chin. "Or maybe I have. Anyway, I keep coming over here, and you've never come over to my place on your own accord. How 'bout it? Would you like to come over?"

"Yes. I would love to come over. Any special time?"

"Anytime you show up will be a special time." He

smiled, and Gwen could see red creeping up from his shirt collar. *He's blushing!* Instantly, he turned and was gone. She smiled and walked to the door to watch him start down the road. She took a deep breath. Her breath was shaky. *Why am I so excited about this? I can't lead him on. I can't lead myself on. I have to keep my ultimate goal in mind. The little red sports car; the little red sports car...*

Gwen went to work cleaning up the kitchen. She had decided to go to town and open a checking account. She also needed to check on moving her savings account from Dallas to the bank in town. She had neglected to do that. She reminded herself that she needed to buy some groceries, dog food, and as an afterthought, decided, *I just might have to buy myself something.*

After Gwen cleaned the kitchen, she went to town, opened a checking account, filled out the papers to have her Dallas savings moved, bought a sandwich at the local coffee shop, and went to the only clothing store in town to get herself a new outfit. Gwen was excited about going to Bo's house. She missed her social life in Dallas, and although this would in no way compare to that, at least it was something. She arrived back at the ranch house, did some laundry, and fed Pal. Time seemed to crawl. She couldn't wait any longer. She showered, shampooed, blew dry, curled her hair, applied make-up for the first time in a long time, and dressed carefully in her new outfit.

While Gwen was driving over to Bo's house, she was in a quandary. She didn't know whether to drive slowly to protect her hairdo or drive fast to get out of the humidity of the August evening and into Bo's air conditioning. Pal ran around in the bed of the truck, lapping at the wind blowing in his face. When Gwen pulled into Bo's driveway, Pal hopped out before she had shut off the engine and ran to meet Roxie. Bo, hearing the truck, walked out to meet Gwen.

Gwen felt ridiculous in her new jeans and Western-style boots. She felt a little pretentious until she saw a mixture of appreciation and admiration cross Bo's face as she approached the porch. "Hey, Dallas, you look really good. After those jeans are washed about twenty times and those boots are half worn out, you'll look *really* good. Yessiree." His eyes traveled up and down her body. He caught himself, clearing his throat. "Hey, come on in here and get out of this heat." She breathed deeply the cool air of the house and looked around the spacious living room.

She had been in the Janway home, but it had been several years ago. When Bo had told her that he bought the place lock, stock, and barrel, she expected that things would be the same. They definitely were not. Hardwood floors had replaced linoleum. Instead of flowered wallpaper, the walls were painted in a soft cappuccino. Gone was the sagging old furniture that had been a part of the Janway home for so long. In its place was a dark brown, buttery-soft leather sectional with suede pillows situated meticulously around it. A rustic native rock fireplace had replaced the wood stove. Western art, along with a collection of western crosses, adorned the walls. One cross in particular caught Gwen's eye. It had been made of barn wood, and holding the cross together was barbed wire. Standing at one end of the sectional was a floor lamp that appeared to be made from a rifle, and a small table that apparently had been made from the same barn wood as the cross. The small table had been decorated with barbed wire also. On the table were a black and white picture of a smiling young lady who bore a remarkable resemblance to Bo and an open Bible.

On the mantel of the new fireplace pranced statuettes of several different breeds of horses.

Instead of the two tiny windows that had been in the back of the living room, French doors led out to a covered patio. *Wow! This is great.* Delicious smells wafted throughout the house. Bo pardoned himself and headed for the kitchen. Gwen started to follow him.

"Do you need any help?"

"No." He guided her back into the living room. "You are my guest, and you will be treated as such." He took her to the sofa and sat her down. "I'll get you something to drink. What do you want?"

"Tea, if you have it."

"I do," he answered and went into the kitchen to get it.

Gwen rose and followed him into the airy kitchen that had been transformed into a cook's delight. Beige tile countertops and back splash, gleaming white appliances and honey oak cabinetry had replaced the Janway's 1950's turquoise and metal. The kitchen ceiling had been removed and opened to reveal the beams above. "This is beautiful."

"Thanks," he answered. "It's a work in progress. Hey, I'm the host here. You go on out to the patio. We're gonna eat out there. It should be cool enough by now. You carry our tea, if you please, and I will be right behind you."

Grudgingly giving up the air conditioning, Gwen made her way to the patio and sat down at the glass-top table. Soon Bo followed.

Bo once again bowed his head to give thanks for the meal, but this time Gwen joined him and thanked God for his many undeserved blessings, including the man across the table who had said a prayer for her when she was hurt.

Bo had fixed a lovely dinner. He had made lasagna, salad, delicious bread, and tea. Gwen felt her jeans becoming tighter, until at last she could hold no more. She leaned back in her chair. "That was delicious, Bo."

"Hold on we're not through. Wait till you see what I have for dessert." He grinned widely.

"Oh no." Gwen groaned. "I can't hold another bite."

"Okay. We can wait awhile. I'll get some coffee, and we can just sit out here."

He went into the house and returned with two cups of coffee. Roxie and Pal were lying in the yard enjoying the coolness of the grass. Gwen and Bo sat on the patio well into the night and talked. He talked about how much feed it would take to feed Gwen's cows, and Gwen talked about what a lovely evening it had been. Finally she stood and stretched. "I guess Pal and I need to go home. I'm tired."

Bo stood. "I wish you didn't have to rush off. We still haven't had our dessert." He smiled that crooked smile that Gwen loved.

She chuckled. "No, we never did, did we? Well, you'll just have to bring it to the house in the morning, and we'll have it for breakfast. I need you to help me make final plans to sell the cattle anyway. Okay?"

"Okay."

Gwen made her way to the truck, and Bo walked with her. When they got to the truck, there was a moment of uncomfortable silence. "Yessir, give those jeans about twenty washings and a couple holes in the knees, and they'll look like they belong to someone who owns a real working cattle ranch." Gwen was embarrassed. She called for Pal, and as soon as he was safely in the back, she hopped in the cab. "Good night. Thanks for dinner, talk, and the company." She waved to him as she backed out of the drive.

She was tired and sleepy but still found time to throw the jeans in the washer and start it before going to bed.

The next morning, Bo brought over an apple pie, and he and Gwen ate big slices with their coffee while they made plans to have the cattle sold.

With Bo's help, within the next few weeks Gwen had accomplished the sale of several head of cattle. She was left with 115 cows, bulls, and calves to care for. With the money from the sale of the cattle and the CD and her car savings safely deposited, Gwen had to admit that she felt much more at ease. Now she had only to buy a few necessities—food and, of course, more jeans.

CHAPTER SEVEN

Gwen and Bo spent a lot of time together and had settled into a comfortable friendship. Gwen knew that if it were not for Bo, she would have given up long ago on running the ranch. Sometimes flirtations passed between them, but Gwen knew they were innocent and nothing would ever come of them. He was just a really good friend. A really good friend who just happened to be male, and a really good-looking, understanding, steady one at that.

September and October went in a flurry of selling cows, buying hay and feed, and getting ready for a long winter. Before Gwen knew it, it was time to make plans for Thanksgiving dinner. T.J. and company were coming and said that they were looking forward to the trip.

Gwen fussed over the old house and wished she had enough money for new furniture or new curtains or new something, but she settled for cleaning everything until it shined and then splurged on a Thanksgiving arrangement of flowers for the kitchen table, which had been moved into the living room to create a dining area.

Bo came over the day before her company arrived, and they sat over coffee and planned dinner. He had paper and pen and a list as long as his gangly arm. He named off different items. Gwen would assure him that she had everything stashed safely away in the refrigerator or cabinets, and everything was going smoothly until he mentioned chicken broth.

"Why do I need chicken broth? I'm having turkey and dressing, not chicken."

"What sort of liquid had you planned on putting in that dressing? How had you planned on making giblet gravy?"

Gwen shrugged. "I didn't. I thought I would let you do that."

"Do you have a chicken we could boil for broth?" he asked, ignoring her comment.

Giving him a childish, innocent look, she slowly shook her head.

"Well"—he jumped up and scooted his chair under the table—"no problem. We'll just run into town and get some broth or a chicken." He slipped his arms into his jacket. "While we're in town, how 'bout a burger?"

"Sounds good to me." She slipped into her denim jacket, grabbed her purse, and started for the door. When she reached the door and realized Bo wasn't behind her, she turned and found him staring at her.

"Yep, I like those jeans more every day."

Gwen grabbed his jacket sleeve and pulled him toward the door, pretending offense. "Let's get to the store before it closes." Inside, though, Gwen's heart was pounding, and her throat was tightening.

A half hour later, Bo pulled up in front of the town's only grocery store and said, "You get what you need; I'll be back in just a second."

As she slid from the seat, he said, "Why don't you get another dozen eggs. You know you can never have too many eggs."

The question, where are you going? was on her lips, but died in the foggy exhaust of the truck as Bo pulled away.

Once in the store, Gwen found the things she needed and headed for the checkout counter. The lines were long with last-minute shoppers, and Gwen wondered if they had all forgotten chicken broth. She let her gaze drift to the darkening parking lot and saw Bo's truck swing into the nearest empty spot. In the beam of his headlights, Gwen could see small snowflakes falling.

Finally her turn came to check out just as she saw Bo come through the door followed by a blast of cold wind. He rubbed his rough hands together and shivered. "Dallas, looks like a blue norther.'" Bo raised his hand, acknowledging a man across the store, "Hey, Red, how goes it?"

Without waiting for an answer, he turned his attention back to Gwen and studied the four sacks of groceries. "Big chicken."

He grabbed two sacks and turned toward the door. Gwen paid for the purchases and picked up the other two sacks.

"I'll get that, ma'am." Gwen looked up at a fresh-faced young boy. She looked out the doors closing behind Bo, then back to the boy.

DONNA BARNARD

"No, thanks. I can manage." She hefted the sacks. Had she ever bought groceries in Dallas, she would never have carried them out herself. Of course, the most she ever bought was a carton of milk, which usually ruined; or a carton of yogurt, which usually ruined.

She hurriedly made her way to the truck. Bo opened the door, and she dumped the two sacks into the front seat and slid in. "It's getting colder. I hope the team makes it up from Dallas. I'm afraid if it's snowing, they won't make it."

Bo started the truck and turned on the windshield wipers. "We won't get much snow."

"How do you know that, Mr. Weatherman? Are your joints not aching, or did you see a caterpillar or something?"

"No," he answered. "See the snowflakes? They're small. Means we won't get much snow."

"Are you sure?"

"Sure, I'm sure. You'll see. Now let's get something to eat. I'm starving."

"Me, too. A hamburger sounds so good right now and a big order of fries and a big—"

"Whoa! You sound like you're gonna founder. Those jeans are tight enough now," he said, laughing.

"Hey, you let me worry about my tight pants. You promised me supper, and I plan on doing some serious eating." Gwen had a mock look of determination on her face. Bo was grinning; he couldn't help but notice Gwen dropping her guard for just a moment.

They drove to the diner at the edge of town and went inside. Bo was greeted by several people, and he introduced Gwen to each in turn. "Oh, yeah, Will's daughter," was a standard response.

"Good to have you back home."

"How've you been, Gwen?"

These were friends of her mom and dad who had known Gwen all of her life, but she didn't know any of the names to fit the faces. As soon as they were seated, a woman with dark knowing eyes and cleavage that looked to Gwen like it went to her kneecaps sloshed two glasses of water in from of them.

"Hi'ya, Bo." She breathed heavily as she leaned over the table with her head propped on her two hands. "What can I do for you?" She emphasized *you* and cut her eyes toward Gwen.

"Hi, Francine. Yes, I'll have a burger basket and a large milk, and Dallas here"—indicating Gwen—"would like a burger basket and…what do you want to drink?" He had to move his head sideways to see around Francine's ample body, which she had practically sprawled across the table.

"I'll have tea…no sugar."

Francine straightened, popped her gum, and made quick notes on her pad. "Gotta watch that figure, huh, sweetie?" She winked at Bo.

"No." Gwen smiled up at her. "I don't have to watch it, but I like the way some other people watch it… *sweetie*." She looked over to Bo and winked. She fluttered her eyelashes and smiled demurely. Francine gave Gwen a look of defiance, turned on her heel, and swayed back behind the counter. Her nose was quite evidently out of joint. Gwen giggled and turned to face Bo, who had an impish grin on his face.

"Dallas," he said in mock disgust, "aren't you ashamed of yourself? Tsk, tsk." He clicked through his teeth.

"I've had better women than that for breakfast and still come away hungry."

"Well, I guarantee you you won't come away hungry from here if you eat what you just ordered." Bo said, changing the subject. "This is Guy's Diner ... home of the Humogoburger."

The jukebox was loudly announcing that some country singer *"wouldn't mind letting a particular woman put her shoes under his bed anytime,"* and smells from the kitchen made Gwen's mouth water. She realized that she hadn't eaten since late morning, and her stomach was harmonizing its own tune to the country song.

"Here you go, Bo." Francine crooned as she placed a large platter in front of him on the table. Then she snickered. "Here you go, Bo. I'm a poet and didn't even know it."

She hastily plunked Gwen's plate down in front of her, and Gwen smiled sweetly up at the waitress. "Thank you so much, Francis," she said in her most condescending tone.

"It's Francine."

"Huh?"

"My name is Francine, not Francis."

"Oh." Gwen looked up apologetically. "Sorry." She shrugged her shoulders.

Francine stalked away, and only then did Gwen look at her platter of food. Her eyes widened, and her mouth dropped when she saw the size of the hamburger that neatly covered half of her platter. The other half of the dish held the largest order of fries Gwen had ever seen. She began calculating calories but lost count.

She glanced over at Bo, who was chuckling. "Told you so."

"I plan on eating every bite of this, so don't bother me." Gwen said, picking up a fry and dipping it in catsup.

"Tonight?" he asked. "Or maybe you were planning on taking it home to snack on for a week?"

"No. When I leave here, there won't be one bite of this left on this plate." With that Gwen began working on the hamburger, which she had to cut into four pieces to better manage it. "To quote a phrase from someone … I plan to divide and conquer." She gave Bo a defiant look.

Bo and Gwen laughed and talked under the icy supervision of the ever-present Francine. Gwen stopped to listen for a moment. The jukebox had stopped. "Bo, would you mind playing some more music?"

"Sure," he said, wiping his mouth with the paper napkin.

Francine, who was watching his every move, intercepted him halfway across the diner, just as Gwen had planned.

"Hey, Bo," she purred, "let me help you pick some real good tunes." She placed one hand on Bo's shoulder as Gwen placed her hand into her fries, scooped up a handful, and dropped them on Bo's platter. She quickly scooped two pieces of her burger into a napkin and placed the bundle in an empty plate on a table next to their booth. No one noticed as she placed another napkin over her ample serving of fries, picked up the bundle, and headed to the ladies' room. When she returned, Bo and Francine were still studying tunes on the jukebox. Gwen noticed that Francine kept touching Bo at every opportunity. Gwen felt jealousy rising and quickly quelled it. After all, she had no ties on him.

As if he felt her eyes on him, Bo turned and threw her a smile. He untangled himself from Francine and strode back to the booth and sat down.

"Well?" he questioned.

"Well what?"

"What do you think of my choice?" She listened and recognized it as the same cheating song that was playing as they entered.

"I think I've heard that one somewhere before. I just imagine *Francis* picked that one, didn't she?"

"Nope. Did that all by myself."

Bo didn't even notice the extra fries on his platter and continued to eat. At last their meal was almost finished, and Gwen drained the last of the tea from her glass.

"I gotta hand it to you, Dallas. You can flat put it away." Bo dragged his napkin across his mouth just as Francine sidled up to the table. "Want somethin' sweet, Bo?"

"Nothing for me, Francine. How about you, Dallas?"

"Do you have any pie?" Gwen asked the gaping front of Francine's uniform.

"Sure, what kind would you like, sweetie?"

"What kind do you have, *sweetie?*"

"Well,"—she stared up at the ceiling, working on her gum—"we got apple, coconut, pecan, cherry, lemon, and egg custard." Her eyes dropped to Gwen.

"What, no chocolate?"

"Nope, no chocolate."

"Well," Gwen drew the words out slowly, "if you don't have chocolate, I guess I don't want any." She turned to look at Bo. "I guess I'm through. I just had my heart set on a big ol' piece of chocolate pie."

She reached down, got her purse, scooted out of the booth and shrugged into her coat then followed Bo to the register. Her jeans were uncomfortably tight, and she felt as though she might never eat another bite of food as long as she lived. As he was paying the tab, Francine leaned over the counter. "When'll *you* be back in town, Bo?"

"Oh, I dunno, Francine. I've been pretty busy lately."

"Busy? Doin' what?" She turned an accusing look to Gwen.

Gwen had had enough of Francine and her gum. She pushed her arm through Bo's. "Come on, Bo. We have to go put *our* groceries away." She smiled amiably and gave Bo's arm a tug.

"Right," he answered with a bemused look. "I'm gone."

He took long strides to the door, and Gwen hurried to keep up.

When the door to the diner shut behind them, he turned and laughed. "I'd better keep some distance between you two."

"I just can't stand it when a woman pushes herself on a man," Gwen said self-righteously.

As they walked to the truck, something occurred to Gwen. "Bo, is Francine your girl? If she is, I don't want to cause any trouble. I'll march right in there and apologize."

"Don't worry about that." He patted Gwen's denim-covered shoulder. "Francine is everybody's girl, if you know what I mean. The only men in this town that she

DONNA BARNARD

doesn't make a pass at is the preacher, who doesn't eat at Guy's, and the town drunk, who doesn't eat. Now get in the truck. I'm freezing." Gwen swung in the truck and felt the warmth where Bo's hand had touched her.

Bo had been right. The snow had stopped, and they drove in comfortable silence through the freezing cold. When they arrived at Gwen's house, Bo helped her in with her sacks and promised to be over early to help her feed and start Thanksgiving dinner.

After he pulled away, loneliness washed over Gwen, but she quickly dismissed it and began putting away what she had bought. As she emptied the bags, she noticed there were five bags instead of the four she remembered having when leaving the grocery store. She reached for the strange bag, peeked inside, and saw a white box. Perplexed, she pulled the box out. It was taped shut. She picked up a knife and snapped the box open. Inside, on top of white tissue paper, was a note written in Bo's scratchy scrawling handwriting.

Maybe this will finish your new look.

She lifted the tissue paper, and inside was a red, western-cut blouse and a leather belt with a shiny silver buckle.

Gwen gasped. The blouse was beautiful, and the thought was even more beautiful.

So that's where he went, she thought as she held up the blouse to better examine it. *Wow, my size too. I'm impressed.*

In a flash, she realized that he would be expecting to see her wearing her new things tomorrow, and she looked down at her one and only pair of jeans. Her fear of running short of money had prevented her from spending any money that she felt wasn't absolutely necessary, and she deemed new Wranglers not really necessary.

"Okay, I'll have to wash these … again." *After all, Bo told me I need to wash them a lot.* She unzipped the jeans and felt immediate relief. *I can't possibly imagine how tightly these would fit if I had actually finished that hamburger.* Slipping out of her boots and sliding her jeans off, she snapped on the washer, threw the jeans in, then decided she had better wash the blouse too. Quickly she removed the tags and threw the new blouse in the washer.

After putting the groceries away, Gwen suddenly realized the house seemed to be getting colder. She stuffed several hunks of wood into the stove, put the kettle on for some tea, picked up Bo's note from the table, and sat down in her mom's creaky rocker, propping her feet toward the heat. Although she was very cold, there was a spot on her shoulder that felt strangely warm. Leaning back, she smiled to herself. In one hand she held Bo's note to her chest, and her other hand touched the spot where just moments before Bo's hand had patted her. Warmth slowly crept throughout her entire body.

DONNA BARNARD

CHAPTER EIGHT

Thanksgiving dawned clear and crackling cold. Gwen padded barefoot to the stove and shoved several pieces of wood on top of the embers left from the night before. *I should carpet this house,* she thought. *Mom and Dad should have carpeted this house and got central heat and air,* she added. As soon as she saw flames licking up the sides of the logs, she rushed around to get ready for the day. She glanced at the clock above the coffee pot. "Seven thirty!" she said aloud. "T.J. and the crew haven't even left Dallas, and here I am in a tizzy. I must be nuts."

Gwen took a quick shower, quicker than usual. She was afraid if she lingered too long she might freeze to death. She wrapped a towel around herself and ran back to the stove to stand in its heat and dry off. "My kingdom for central heat," she said through chattering teeth.

Sun was peeping through the windows at the front

of the house, and she shuffled to pull the curtains wide. Her eyes fell absently on the front yard. Frost covered everything. Trees that yesterday seemed bleak and dead had come to life overnight. A light breeze put small limbs in motion to create a dazzling myriad of colors.

For a long moment, Gwen was entranced by the theatrics that Mother Nature had created and felt that the show was just for her. A shotgun blast sliced through the cold stillness and brought her cruelly back to reality.

"Oh, for Pete's sake! Deer hunters! Don't they even stay home for Thanksgiving?"

Another shot.

"Obviously not." She turned away from the window.

Hurrying, she trotted back through the house, grabbed what clothes she needed from the bedroom, and made her way back to the stove to get dressed. She pulled on the pink thermal underwear that she had worn when she and the gang from T. J.'s had gone to Aspen the winter before. She drew a fleece robe on over the thermal underwear.

She stuffed her new blouse and jeans in the dryer. That would feel nice ... warm clothes.

The rocker was still sitting where she had left it the night before, so Gwen poured herself a cup of coffee, pulled her robe tightly around her, and hugged her legs to her chest. She closed her eyes. The crackle of the fire, the clatter of the brass buttons and snaps in the dryer, the creak of the ancient chair; it was so peacef— Another shot rang out. This one at least seemed farther away. "Ugh!"

A quick glance at the clock told her that Bo would soon be there to help feed. Gwen drew her knees up closer; barring noisy deer hunters, she still had a few minutes of solitude and coffee before Bo would be there, or so she thought. Gwen heard Bo's truck as it crunched through the frozen low-water crossing. Pal barked a welcome, and Gwen jumped up, throwing off her robe and grabbing her dad's old coverall's from the coat rack. Bo never came into the house until after all the chores had been done, so Gwen just pulled on rubber boots and dashed out the door to meet him.

Pal had beaten her to the truck and was already wagging a welcome.

Gwen pushed open the heavy metal gate and quickly discovered that she had failed to put on gloves. The question of temperature ran through her mind as Bo eased through the opening, flashing her a one-sided smile. Her heart skipped a beat as she smiled back.

She pulled her gloves from her pocket and loped to the barn.

"Mornin,' sunshine." Bo smiled through a frosty fog. "Know what the temperature is?"

"No," she answered while opening the gate to the hay barn. "Do you?"

"Thirteen," he exclaimed. "Thirteen, and it's just Thanksgiving. Can't imagine what it's going to be by January."

They loaded the truck with feed and hay, and Gwen jumped behind the wheel. She slowly pulled the truck from the barn and headed out to the pasture. As soon as the cows heard the truck, they began bawling in anticipation. Gwen drove in a large circle, and Bo snapped wires and tossed the hay from each side of the truck. When they had finished, Bo flung the passenger-side door open and hopped into the truck. "Too cold to ride in the back."

Gwen slowly made her way to the feed troughs where Bo poured the feed, trying to distribute it equally.

This had been their routine every morning for the past three weeks. Bo told her she could do it by herself after she got the hang of it, but he continued to come morning after morning.

Feed sacks and baling wires stored, Gwen drove back into the yard while Bo held the gate open for her. After she shut the truck engine off, she invited him in for coffee. "Might as well; I have to put Tom in to cook anyhow." Their feet crunched as they stepped on the crispy grass. "Go ahead. I'll feed Pal, then I'll be in."

"No," she answered. "I'll feed Pal. You just fed the cows. You go on in and pour us some coffee, and I'll be in in just a minute."

Gwen reached into a large barrel and dug out a pan of food for Pal, who had left his warm bed to help feed. "Here you go, boy. When you finish this, I may invite you in to warm by the stove."

Bo was taking care of the fire when Gwen came in. She slid out of her rubber boots and started to unzip the coveralls before remembering that the only thing she had on under the coveralls was thermal underwear. "Go ahead and build up that fire. I'll be back in just a jiff."

After going to her bedroom and removing the coveralls, she walked back to the living room wearing her bathrobe. "Before I forget it, thanks for the gift. The blouse and belt are just perfect." She felt strangely embarrassed just mentioning it.

"Oh, my gosh! Did I bring those in here? I bought

those for Francine. I guess I brought them in here by mistake."

Gwen raised one eyebrow and smirked. "Yeah, I'll bet Francine could fit in that blouse."

Bo grinned and nodded in agreement. He went to work immediately getting the turkey ready for roasting, and Gwen just sat and watched as he deftly went through the steps. When he had the turkey settled comfortably in the oven, he joined Gwen at the table with a cup of coffee. "When's this crew of yours supposed to be here?"

"They should arrive around two o'clock; that is, if they don't get lost. I sent T.J. a detailed map, but you never know. "

"She's not too good at reading a map, huh?"

"I don't know about her map-reading skills. She's actually been here before. She came out here after Dad's funeral but that's been awhile, and if you don't know where you're going, it's a little difficult to find your way out here, you know."

Bo rose and stretched. "Yep, I know that. That's the main reason I bought the Janway place."

"Well, don't worry about Tom there." He indicated the oven. "He'll be fine. I'm going to run home and shower and get ready for your big-city friends. I'll be back before you know it. If you want to do anything, just set the table. Don't try to cook anything," he teased.

"Thanks for the vote of confidence."

"I know the facts, lady," he said, tweaking her cheek. "And the fact is, you can't cook. If you could, you would have already done so. Well, I'll be back pretty quick with pumpkin pies." He jammed his stocking cap down over his ears and strode out the door. "Bye." He waved to her as he crunched across the yard. *One of these days I'll show you how I can't cook, mister!*

Perfect, she thought, *now I can get ready too.* She deposited the cups in the sink and rushed to the bathroom. She ran to the dryer for her clothes. They were still warm. She flattened her jeans across the bed and slung the new red blouse on a hanger.

She knew that Bo would be back shortly, so she hurriedly took a shower, brushed her hair until it shined and pulled it up into a side-swinging ponytail. She let a few tendrils hang loose around her face. She wanted to look nice for Bo, but she also wanted to look fashionable for her friends. She dumped her makeup out on the bathroom cabinet and had to stop to think about what went on first. She laughed at herself. "Been a long time, huh?" She shrugged her shoulders and began to plop, dollop, and smear.

The end product was not too bad, she surmised, and with one arm, she pulled everything back into the makeup case. She plugged in the curling iron and went to the bedroom to get dressed. Afterward Gwen checked herself in a full-length mirror and was pleased with what she saw. The belt and the blouse were perfect, and she mentally thanked Bo again. She rushed back to the bathroom, put a few curls in the ponytail, and curled the tendrils a bit. Finished with herself, she ran through the house and made sure that everything was still as neat as possible. She had just hung the coveralls back on the coat rack when she heard Bo's truck.

She quickly brushed an imaginary fluff of lint from the blouse and stood stiffly in front of the door.

"Hey, Dallas, open up!"

She flung the door wide, and there stood Bo. He

had on stiffly starched blue jeans, a denim jacket, a red and black plaid shirt, black boots, and an ancient black felt hat. Gwen's heart gave a lurch. She blinked several times and closed her mouth after realizing it was hanging open. She had never seen him in anything except work clothes.

"Hey, you gonna let me in?" He was standing on the porch with two pies still smoking in the cold morning air.

"Oh, sorry." She pushed the screen door open and let him pass through. She couldn't take her eyes off him as he came through the door, and she continued to watch as he made his way across the living room and disappeared into the kitchen. Gwen decided the view from the back was just as impressive as the view from the front. He went straight to an already crowded cabinet and deposited the pies. He walked back into the living room to stand in front of the woodstove.

"I'll tell you, those pies are still pretty hot ... say, speaking of hot, lady, you look great." He briskly rubbed his hands together and made his way back to the kitchen.

Gwen was still standing, holding the door open. "So do you," she mumbled.

"What?" he called from the kitchen.

"They sure smell good," Gwen said, following him toward the kitchen.

Bo turned and looked her over. "That blouse is perfect," he said. "I thought maybe you would look good in red. And that belt ... hey, it looks really familiar." He grinned and looked down at his own. Gwen's was a small replica of his. "No wonder I like that belt so much." He grinned again.

"Oh, I love it"—Gwen stumbled for words—"I, uh, I love it ... and I well, you know ... and I, uh, and I love the blouse too." She suddenly had an urge to give him a hug, and since she had never been one to deny an urge, she moved to him and circled her arms around his neck. On impulse, she pulled back and planted a kiss on his cheek. "Thanks again," she said, suddenly feeling shy.

Bo's usual ruddy complexion had turned a shade much like the cranberry sauce chilling in the refrigerator.

"You're welcome," he muttered, quickly turning toward the oven. "I guess I need to check on Thomas," he added, rushing back into the kitchen.

CHAPTER NINE

The rest of the morning was spent with the two of them preparing Thanksgiving dinner. Gwen was awestruck that a man could show such expertise in the kitchen. The mixture of aromas that permeated the old house were making Gwen's mouth water, and by two o'clock, when her guests still had not arrived, she was ready to say to heck with them and go ahead and eat. She was extremely hungry. She suggested that they grab a glass of tea and retire to the living room. Being both tired and hungry, they literally fell onto the comfy old sofa.

Bo admitted that he was as tired as he would have been if he had been building fence all day. He studied Gwen for moment. "Hey," he questioned, "how come women feel like they have to wear all that stuff on their faces? I think you look just fine without—"

"Oh, they're here." Gwen jumped up when she heard a car in the driveway and Pal barking a fake warning. At least, Gwen thought it was a fake warning until she opened the door and saw Pal, standing on the porch with his hackles raised and teeth bared. She laughed at the way he was seemingly stalking a new and tasty prey.

T.J. piled out of her large black Cadillac in all her sophisticated glory and lifted both fur-covered arms in a "we finally made it" sign. Her black hair was pulled severely upward into a bun at the top of her head. Her makeup was perfect, and she was wearing diamond earrings and a necklace to match and, in Gwen's opinion, terribly uncomfortable-looking heels. *Never let it be said that T. J. is one to overdress!* Not thinking of the cold, Gwen ran out of the house into her arms.

T.J. moved back and held Gwen at arm's length. "Oh, dearie," she said, in a soft Texas drawl. "You look so … so … *country.*" She spun Gwen around. "You've lost weight … and you've been in the sun. You're gonna to do just dreadful things to your skin." She finally noticed Gwen's teeth chattering. "And you're freezin'! Let's get inside."

"Lance, Kaycee, do be dears and get out. Let's get this child in the house before she freezes." T.J. was addressing her two passengers, who were warily crawling from T.J.'s car.

They were eying Pal as if he were the local grizzly, ready to pounce and do them bodily harm. Gwen laughed and called to Pal to come to her.

"He won't hurt you. Come on in." Pal gave his famous doggy grin and trotted over to stand beside her.

Kaycee and Lance were two of T.J.'s top designers and looked every bit the part of the stereotypical fashion designers. Lance wore a gray tweed overcoat thrown over narrow shoulders. Under the coat he wore a pink silk shirt and gray silk-blend trousers. His narrow feet were housed in rich-grained alligator shoes. His blonde hair was pulled back tightly and caught at the nape of his neck in a ponytail. His lips were a shade of blue to match his eyes and the circles beneath them.

Kaycee, on the other hand, was dressed in a mini-skirt, leggings, knee-high boots, and a cashmere tunic, with a wool scarf draped around her neck. She was wearing too much lipstick, too much black eye makeup, and her jet-black hair was parted in the center and hung past her thin shoulders. In one ear hung a diamond cross. She always appeared to have something unpleasant permanently attached to her upper lip. She had a hair-trigger temper, and even though Lance and Kaycee had been friends and co-designers for many years, their arguments were the talk of the trade.

T.J. and Gwen walked arm-in-arm to the porch. Pal growled deeply as T.J. started up the steps. "My good-ness," she said. "Hush, dawg, you just *think* I'm wearin' one of your cousins." She leaned in toward Pal. "Don't tell anyone, but it's not real. I don't wear real." Once on the porch, she turned to Kaycee and Lance. "Listen, don't y'all come outside without Gwennie. I feel this dog might just be able to do some major damage ... and enjoy doin' it." She threw her head back and laughed. Gwen smiled at her teasing remarks.

The two swerved around Pal, and Pal, sensing their fear, took advantage of the situation by growling deeper and longer as he watched every move the two made. Gwen couldn't help but notice it appeared that Pal was grinning all the while. She laughed as the two came up on the porch. "Don't laugh, Gwennie. A dog bite can be a serious thing," whined Kaycee.

Gwen released T.J.'s arm and placed herself between the dog and Kaycee and Lance. She turned, wagging her finger toward Pal. "Pal, these are my friends. If you want to assert your authority, go find a wolf or something." She smiled wickedly.

"A w-wolf!" stammered Kaycee.

"Or something?" asked Lance. Both scanned the front yard and quickly followed Gwen into the house.

T.J. had stopped just inside the door and was looking over the living room. "Oh, Gwennie, you poor child. What have you endured for these past months? You've been livin' in these primitive surroundings ... and you've got more to go. I thought at least you'd buy new furniture or ... something ... at least. " She whirled around to face Gwen. "I'm sorry that I ever suggested you stay. You must be miserable. I'm so sorry. This place is not worth the trials you must be goin' through. Pack right now," she said with a flourish, "and come back to Dallas with us. We'll help you pack, huh, guys?"

"Ghastly," observed Kaycee.

"Ugh," was Lance's only opinion as he wiped imaginary dust from his hands.

Gwen found herself bristling.

T.J. rattled on. "We could leave right now except that I'm famished, and the smells comin' from your kitchen are makin' my mouth water." She threw the faux fur carelessly across the sofa and took off toward the kitchen but stopped short and began backing into the living room. Bo followed her out of the kitchen with his hand outstretched. "Howdy," he drawled. "I'm

DONNA BARNARD

Bo Bohanan, *Gwennie's* neighbor." Gwen noticed the emphasis that he placed on her pet name.

"Oh, yeah, in the excitement, I forgot. This is my neighbor, Bo ... Bo, this is T.J"—Gwen noticed that T.J. appeared to be enjoying the view—"and Kaycee,"—who was drooling—"and Lance," who looked incredulous. As Gwen introduced each of her friends, she noticed that Bo's eyes lingered for a moment over each.

"Well, that's over with. Come on, I'll show you where to wash up and where you will be sleeping." Gwen took off down the hallway, leading her small parade.

She showed T.J. and Kaycee into her mom and dad's bedroom, and they tentatively stepped in. Gwen showed Lance into her bedroom. "This is where you will be sleeping. This was my bedroom when I was a child."

"Oh my goodness, you lived such a deprived childhood. How did you stand it? Oh, by the way, where is the neighbor sleeping? You know what they say about loving thy neighbor," he added lasciviously. Gwen ignored both comments and handed him a hanger.

"Maybe you should get out of your coat and hang it up; then we can get ready to eat. I imagine that you are all pretty hungry. Bo has worked all morning cooking this wonderful meal."

"Bo?" From the hallway, T.J. looked incredulous. She walked into Gwen's bedroom, followed by Kaycee. She lowered her voice. "That guy cooked our meal? Gwennie, are you sure this is what you want to do? I can't believe this is where you're meant to be or that this is the best path for your life right now. I just don't think this cowboy is what you need in your life. If you're gonna have a *friend*, why not pick one that would have been a little more socially acceptable?" She rolled her eyes.

That was all Gwen could take. "Bo *is* socially acceptable in *his* society—*our* society. Hey, it was you that encouraged me to live here. Remember the speech about being just where I'm supposed to be, and for your information,"—she wagged her head—"he is not a *friend*. Not in the way you're insinuating. He's my neighbor and a good one at that. He has helped me practically every day that I have been here. He is sweet, kind, and generous to a fault. I would have given up in the first week if it hadn't been for Bo. He's my friend, and I'll thank you to keep your opinions to yourself."

"Sorry, darlin.' Calm down. What are you, in love or something? I'm just worried about you being up here so far from your friends. Is he a good Christian man? Have you asked him what his intentions are toward you?" T. J. reached out and gently patted Gwen on the forearm.

"No," answered Gwen more calmly as she counted off the answers on her fingers. "I'm not in love. He is just a very good friend. Yes, he is a good Christian man. A better Christian than I am. As a matter of fact, he's taught me quite a lot about how to be a good Christian. And at this point, his intentions haven't been a problem. He has been nothing but honorable in my presence." She took a long breath and let it out slowly as she looked from one guest to another. "I'm sorry. I'm just so glad to see you, and I want y'all to have a wonderful time while you're here." She threw her arms around all of them.

"Forget it." T.J. wagged her hand back and forth, as if brushing the disagreement away. "It's not the first time we've disagreed on something." She looked up at Kaycee and Lance, who were, grinning foolishly from the doorway where they now stood. "I am starving. Let's go eat. I didn't come all this way for a fight. I came to see how you are doing. I love you, Gwennie, and I worry about you. Now can we please eat? I'm starvin'!"

CHAPTER TEN

Gwen asked Bo if he would give thanks. After his short but heartfelt prayer, she looked over at T. J. who was smiling, blinking in amazement.

Dinner went well, even through a forced amicability. Lance kept eyeing Bo as though at any moment he might do something totally inappropriate, and Kaycee kept looking at him as if she was hoping he would.

T.J. placed small amounts of food on her plate and refused the fluffy potatoes and the rich steaming giblet gravy. She almost placed some corn on her plate and then silently shook her head, apparently talking herself out of it. Gwen piled generous helpings of everything that came her way and reached for two huge yeast rolls and began smearing them with liberal amounts of real butter. The table was strangely silent except for the sound of Bo's spoon scraping up a last bit of gravy. Gwen looked up to see T.J. and company staring wide-

DONNA BARNARD

eyed at her plate. "Does someone have a comment to make?" she asked.

"No, no, not at all," Kaycee answered. Lance just raised his eyebrows and looked down at his plate.

"Well, I have a comment," said T.J.

"I thought you might."

"Gwennie, if you continue to eat like a cow, you will find yourself looking like one. You must be careful, or that perfect size six will become a perfect size twice that ... or more."

"You let me worry about my figure. I've been eating like this lately, and I haven't gained one ounce. As a matter of fact, you said yourself that I looked like I had lost weight. I work hard, and I use up a lot of energy."

No more was said, and the rest of the meal was eaten under a strained silence.

Bo rose from the table. "I'll get the pie."

"I'll help," Gwen quickly said.

Bo and Gwen returned with a tray filled with generous slices of pumpkin pie. On top of each piece was an enormous dollop of whipped cream.

T.J. carefully scraped the whipped cream off and cut a sliver of pie from her piece.

Gwen, after sitting down, studied her piece of pie then rose, picked it up, and disappeared back into the kitchen. "Good girl, Gwennie," said T.J. "Forego the dessert. You'll love yourself for it."

Gwen went to the cabinet, spooned more whipped cream on top of her pie, and returned to the table. "I love myself pretty much just as I am," she said and opened wide. After saying it, she realized that she sounded snide. This was the Dallas side of Gwen. This was the defiant, self-absorbed Gwen. Not the rancher

Gwen. She glanced over at Bo, who was busy working on a piece of pie himself, but thought she detected the slightest hint of a smile around the corners of his over-stuffed mouth.

After dinner they had coffee. T. J. and Bo seemed to hit it off right away. T. J. drilled Bo with questions, as was her habit with people she didn't know. "Oh," Gwen heard her say, obviously impressed, "you're an attorney." Gwen smiled and returned to studying her guests. Lance and Kaycee were sitting together on the old sofa. Their faces revealed how ill at ease they were. Every few minutes each of them squirmed as if looking for a more comfortable location on the sagging sofa. Each time wood was added to the woodstove, Lance would give a little cough expressing his displeasure, and Kaycee would wrinkle her nose. Gwen couldn't help but notice how uncomfortable Kaycee and Lance appeared to be. T. J., on the other hand, was completely undaunted, as she usually was; but the conversation between Lance, Kaycee, and the others was strained, and even small amenities appeared unnatural. Finally Lance rose and quietly disappeared toward the back of the house. A few minutes later, Kaycee followed.

Since the weather had turned so cold, Bo and Gwen had been feeding hay morning and evening, so at four o'clock Bo rose and lifted his coat from the rack. "Gotta go do my chores. I'll come back to help you do yours," he spoke to Gwen. Obviously in a hurry, he stepped through the door. Kaycee and Lance returned to the living room. It was as if someone had removed the stopper. Words began to flow from all three of the guests at once.

"Oh my God, Gwennie. You can't possibly stay

here. This place is atrocious. Leave here today," begged Lance.

"Stop." Gwen jumped up, boiling. All that she had withheld during dinner came pouring out. "This is my home. I was born here. My roots are here, and I plan on staying here until my year is up. At that time I will let you know whether or not I plan on returning to Dallas. I may, and I may not. And you,"—she indicated Lance and Kaycee—"are snobs. Bo worked hard to make that dinner special for all of us. The very least you could have done was thank him. T. J. was accepting of him, and I heard her tell him what a wonderful meal he had prepared. I am ashamed of you two. I'm more ashamed of myself for not speaking up while he was still here. He is so much better than you two. Pardon me." She made her way to the coat rack and began pulling on coveralls and slipping into rubber boots. "I have chores to do. Make yourselves at home,"—she spat the words at the two who were now clinging to each other— "if you think that's possible." She turned to T. J. and smiled. "I'll be back as soon as I take care of things." She threw a look of disgust to the cringing couple as she jerked the door open and stalked through.

Once outside, the cold air hit her full force, and she pulled on her gloves as she stepped off the porch. Padding behind her was Pal; he grinned up at Gwen, and at once her anger faded. "Now what?" she asked him. "The best I can do by myself is feed you. Are you hungry?" He answered with a wag of his stubby tail.

Gwen dug a pan full of feed from the barrel, placed it on the porch, and gave Pal a loving rub on the head. He eagerly began eating. Standing looking out toward the barn, she wondered what else she could do to release some of the steam building inside her. She turned and walked to the old pickup, jumped in, and started it. It coughed, sputtered for a moment, then purred into action. She ground the gears down and drove to the metal gate. She didn't have a plan; she was just acting on impulse. She hopped out of the truck, opened the gate, and drove through. Once inside the pasture, she reversed her actions to close the gate. Then she drove to the barn.

She backed the truck through the double doors of the barn, backing as close to the bales of hay as possible. Hopping down from the cab, she lowered the tailgate and began loading bales into the back of the truck. When she had finished, she made sure the wire cutters were in the truck and pulled out into the pasture. She stopped just outside the doors and ran quickly to close them. The cows had heard the truck and were making their ways down off the mountain, bawling in anticipation.

She ran back to the cab of the truck. *I'm off to feed my cows. My cows,* she thought. *My cows.*

She drove to the same area where she and Bo had distributed hay just that morning. She stopped, dropped down out of the cab, and crawled into the bed of the truck. Quickly she began snapping wires. The ever-hungry cattle began moving closer. She threw hay from both sides of the truck and over the tailgate. Then she jumped down, got back in the cab, and did it all over again until all of the hay was gone.

The work, the solitude, and the cold had worked a miracle on her state of mind, and she felt good. She breathed in the cold air. It hurt her lungs, but it purged her soul. She stared up at the blue-gray sky. "Thank you, Lord, for this wonderful day of Thanksgiving. Thank you for Bo and T. J. and even Kaycee and Lance and cows and my wonderful dog." She looked around but couldn't see Pal anywhere.

As she pulled the truck back toward the barn, from the corner of her eye she caught a movement. Turning, she saw Pal running across the pasture toward the truck. "Hey, old man, did you come to help? If you did, you're a little late, but I appreciate it all the same." As he neared the truck, he cowered down. If he had had a tail, it would have been between his legs. "What's the matter? I'm not mad at you."

She was dreading going back into the house anyway, so she decided that she would just sit and talk to Pal for a while. She killed the engine and opened the door of the truck. "Come up here and see me." Immediately, he brightened and hopped into the truck.

Gwen dug her fingers into his thick coat and rubbed him all over. He was ecstatic. She let her mind run back to the tirade. "Was I too rough on them, Pal? I guess I just lost my temper." Gwen continued to pat and rub. Pal jumped from the cab and took his usual seat in the bed of the truck. Gwen slid from the truck, climbed up on the tailgate, and sat down next to him. "Did you hear what I said about maybe not returning to Dallas? I really don't know why I said that. I have always intended to return to Dallas. Haven't I?" She turned to Pal, as if expecting an answer. He smiled at her and cocked one ear to ask if she was going to continue rubbing. Gwen smiled back to him and ruffed his ears. She sat in silence, running her hand absently down his spine. Suddenly, Pal raised his head and looked toward the stream that ran through the pasture. Gwen swung her head around. Standing on the bank was a doe and two yearlings. She supposed they were her fawns from last spring. Warily, they approached the water and drank. Gwen sat in fascination watching. As they drank, one deer was constantly on guard duty. As the guard dropped its head, another would assume watch.

The ethereal beauty of the scene took her breath away. The setting sun drenched the naked frosty trees in blazing light. Not a sound could be heard except for the munching of the contented cattle. Gwen sat in awe.

The three deer, in unison, raised their heads, ears twitching and tails standing high for a moment before disappearing into the trees. Gwen looked around to see if she could determine what had scared them away but could see nothing. Shortly she heard Bo's truck rattling down the road.

"How about that, Pal? The deer heard Bo coming, and from the look of that sorry excuse you have for a tail, so did you. "

Jumping down from the bed of the truck, she said to the ever-present dog, "Pal, how about you riding up front with me? It's really cold out here." She threw the door open and motioned for him to get in. He didn't need a second invitation. On the drive back from the barn, she was rewarded with several dog kisses. As Gwen drove around the barn and headed toward the house, she noticed that the driveway was empty. T.J.'s Cadillac was gone!

DONNA BARNARD

CHAPTER ELEVEN

T.J., Kaycee, and Lance had returned to Dallas. Gwen was informed of this fact by a note, which she found under a magnet on the refrigerator door. The letter had been scrawled quickly by T. J. She stood, still in her coveralls and read:

> G,
>
> *Sorry to rush off without saying goodbye, but I have been out-voted. L and K want to get back to civilization, as they put it. You're doing a wonderful job with the ranch, and I am very proud of the work that you've done here. Don't pay any attention to what I said about leaving the ranch. I only said it to get your reaction, and the reaction I got proved that I was right all along. I still believe that you are here because you're supposed to be. I feel deeply that God has placed Bo in your life for a divine purpose. Don't fight it, darlin,' just enjoy your time here. Tell Bo that I really enjoyed meeting him. He's a wonderful cook, a very intelligent*

man, and I really liked talking to him. Whatever you decide to do, I'm with you 100%. Call me, and we'll have a nice long visit. And, G, I'm counting on you coming to Dallas for the Christmas holidays.

Love, T. J.

When Gwen heard Bo knocking on the door, she opened it, and as he entered, she handed him the note.

"I'm sorry," Bo sympathized. "I know what plans you had and how much you were looking forward to this visit from your friends. But if you want to go to Dallas for Christmas, I'll be happy to take care of things while you're gone. That's no problem."

"Friends! With friends like those two, I don't need any enemies."

Bo stepped closer. He placed his hands on her shoulders and let his hands slide slowly down until Gwen's hands were in his. "You always have me," he said gently. Gwen knew even before looking that he would have that mischievous look on his face.

She raised her burning eyes to his. "Yes." She smiled. "I have you and Pal and Apple and the co—"

He leaned forward, and for a fleeting moment, Gwen was petrified that he was going to kiss her; at the same time, she was afraid he wouldn't. He tentatively brushed his lips across her cheek.

He pulled away, and just for a second, Gwen could see indecision flash through his eyes. He suddenly drew back and dropped her hands. "Well," he said too loudly, "I see that you're ready to do chores. I guess we'd better get busy." He started walking to the door.

"I've already done the chores."

He turned quickly. "*You* did the chores?"

"Yes."

"You hayed the cows!"

"Yes."

He had started walking toward her. The look on his face was almost one of anger.

"You put the hay out alone?"

"Yes."

"You drove the truck?"

"Yes."

"How did you manage? That hay is heavy!"

She shrugged. "I managed."

He was now dangerously close.

Once again he laid his hands on her shoulders. His grip tightened. He stopped and looked deeply into her eyes. Her heart lurched.

Then his face broke into a broad grin. "Lady, you are something else." His grip eased. He patted her on the back, and she felt the same as when her first grade teacher had told her that her crayon picture was the best picture she had ever seen.

Bo dropped his hands to his sides and turned toward the kitchen. "Okay," he said, rubbing his hands together. "You did the chores,"—he removed his coat and began rolling up his shirtsleeves—"so I'll clean up the kitchen."

"No, no," she protested. "That's a big job. I'll help." She started removing her coveralls.

"All right," he agreed. "Then I'll take you out to supper. No hamburgers, though. How 'bout it?"

"We're not going to find anything open tonight. It's Thanksgiving, remember? How about I fix our supper right here?"

"You're gonna cook?"

"Hey now, be nice. I'm not just a ranch foreman, you know."

"No, you're not. But I still need to get this kitchen cleaned."

"I'll help, and the work will go really quickly. How 'bout that?"

"You've got a deal."

Together they began cleaning the kitchen. As they were putting all the leftovers away, Bo observed, "Just think, for the next two weeks, we won't have to go out to eat. We can have turkey salad, turkey sandwiches, turkey casserole, turkey burgers, turkey surprise ... and turkey."

CHAPTER
TWELVE

After the kitchen chores were done, the two decided that since neither was very hungry, they would just have salads and tea.

After eating, Bo left for home, saying he was calling it a night because he was really tired. Gwen admitted that she, too, was tired. As soon as Bo left, she fell promptly into bed. She was exhausted but felt much better about T.J. and company leaving without notice. She lay in the bed for a long time, thinking about the day. She remembered the way Pal had acted when he came to the truck while she was feeding the stock. She remembered the way he cowered. Suddenly, Gwen was angry. "Lance," she growled. She visualized him doing all sorts of things to the hapless dog. She began getting angrier. She lay in the bed and tried to imagine herself doing all sorts of things to Lance. She was staring up at the ceiling, listening to the silence around her, when in the distance to the southwest just barely she heard the rumble of thunder. "I hope it's raining in Dallas, and I hope it's raining on his perfectly styled hair." She spoke into the darkness. Those words were that last thing she remembered until the sun shined through her window to wake her.

The month between Thanksgiving and Christmas was amazingly short, and before she realized it, it was time for her to begin thinking about going to Dallas for Christmas. She had more or less promised T.J. that she would think about it. She was sitting in front of the woodstove; her socked feet propped up taking advantage of the heat. She *was* thinking about it. She rose and went to the window that looked across the pasture to the mountain that ran the length of her ranch. *My ranch,* she thought. *My ranch.*

This is winter in Oklahoma. "Beautiful," she said aloud. The scene was both beautiful and stark. The leaves were gone from the hardwoods, and the only things that were green were the cedars and loblolly pine.

The quiet was almost deafening. The sun reflecting from the heavy frost that clung to the sleeping grass and the winter-blackened trees turned the picture of bleakness into a picture from a fairy tale. It looked as though everything were covered with diamond dust. She drew her winter robe closer in an effort to ward off the cold. Grudgingly, she forced her thoughts back to the present. A glance at the clock told her that Bo would be pulling in at any moment to help feed. "It's beautiful all right, 'til you have to get out in it and then it's *cold!*" She gulped down the remainder of her coffee.

She donned her heaviest clothes and walked out on the porch. Her breath formed clouds of mist around her face. The cold was biting and yet invigorating. She ran her fingers through Pal's thick winter coat and felt ice crystals break away. "It's really cold this morning, isn't it?" Pal answered with a wag of this stubby tail and a toothy grin.

Gwen heard Bo's truck coming up the road as she headed to the gate to open it for him. Pulling through the gate, Bo smiled a good morning. Gwen pulled the gate shut and ran to the pickup as she normally did. She hopped up in the bed of the truck. Bo knocked on the back glass and indicated that she should get in. She jumped down and ran shivering to the cab.

The warmth of the truck felt good. "Mornin,' sunshine," he drawled. "How do you like this weather?" Without waiting for an answer, he added. "Guess what the temperature is?" He still didn't wait for an answer. "It's nine degrees. Nine degrees!"

Gwen shivered. "I knew it felt colder than usual."

"This isn't really normal for this time of year. This is more like January weather. Looks like we're in for a long, hard winter. 'Bout time, though. We haven't had a really bad winter for several years now."

And it had to be this year.

They reached the barn, and Bo backed into the darkness of the hall.

They both left the warmth of the pickup and together started putting the hay on the truck.

"I guess we'd better give them some extra today. They're going to need it. I heard on the weather this morning that this cold front is here to stay for a while." With each breath, clouds of vapor puffed around his face. Gwen could feel her nose running and freezing at the same time.

"I'm going to give them some extra cubes this morning too." He talked over his shoulder as he walked to the feed room. "Hey, Dallas, you need to stock up on feed. You only have enough for this morning." He came out of the feed room carrying a fifty-pound sack of feed under each arm. "We need to go to the feed store today." He threw the sacks of feed on the tailgate of the truck and turned to get more. "You might look to see what you need in the way of food for yourself. We may be in for a spell."

Gwen remembered fondly when, as a child, the many days through the winter when school was closed because of snow or ice. She reveled in the mini-vacation and played in the snow, sledding, and building snowmen.

Bo continued to throw his words from the feed room. All Gwen could do was listen and shiver. Her teeth were chattering too hard to talk. Bo brought out two more sacks of feed and placed them next to the first two. He looked at Gwen sitting atop the hay. "Why don't you get in the truck while I finish this? I just need one more." While she crawled down from the hay, Gwen was silently thanking him.

After loading the feed and hay, Bo swung into the truck. He rubbed his gloved hands together before taking the wheel. "Dallas," he said, "you're out of cubes. I used all you had. We'll go get some today. I need some too, so we'll just take both trucks." He put the truck in gear and pulled out of the barn. "I'll come by, and we can go together. I may even treat you to a bowl of chili." *I could use a good hot bowl of chili to soak my feet in right about now.* "You sure are quiet this morning. What are you thinking about?"

"The weather," she answered truthfully. She was thinking that the weather had made up her mind for her concerning the trip to Dallas for Christmas. There was no way she could go now and leave all this work for Bo. The weather had given her an excuse, and she felt relief that she had such a handy one. After all, Bo had his own ranch to look after, and she felt guilty enough about having his help every day. She couldn't go off and leave all of her work for him too. She made a mental note to send T.J. a Christmas card with her apologies for not being able to come to Dallas to spend the holiday.

When they drove down into the pasture, some of the cattle began running to the truck. They were hungry. *How much feed will I need?* she wondered. *How much will it cost?*

"Bo, how much feed do you suppose I will need?" She spoke from the driver's seat after Bo had gotten out to put feed in the troughs.

"I'll figure that out later, but for right now, let's just the rest of the chores done so we can get in the house and have a cup of coffee. How 'bout it? My chin and cheeks are freezing off."

"I'm all for that," she said but was thinking what a shame it would be for those lips to freeze off. She threw him a smile, hoping he couldn't read her thoughts.

She felt much better noticing that his nose was running and freezing also.

"What we can't haul, the feed store will deliver for us." Bo continued, oblivious of her thoughts, "If they can get out here. So don't worry about not being able to haul it."

Actually, that wasn't what she was worried about.

Gwen was worried about buying so much that she couldn't pay for it. The money from the sale of the cattle, the CD, and the car savings were dwindling fast. Because of the drought, the hay had been extremely expensive, and since the first frost, she had been feeding hay and cubes every day. *I think I need to get rid of my apartment. I'm still paying rent in Dallas, and each month that's coming out of my car savings. At this point, I'm not even sure I'll ever see Dallas again.*

She was lost in thought when Bo yelled from the back of the truck. "Okay, start the hay circle!" She pulled to the area where they put the hay out every morning and afternoon. Gwen drove in a large arch, while Bo threw out the hay.

Gwen watched in the rearview mirror to make certain when to stop for the cutting of another bale. When all of the hay was out, Bo banged on top of the truck for her to stop. Instead of getting in on the driver's side, he slid in on the passenger's side. "You drive. My hands are too cold. I can hardly feel my fingers, and my mouth and chin have disappeared. I can't feel them anymore. Gwen looked at his full lips and thought again how sad that would be if they were no more. She shook her head to shake away her thoughts. "Let's go!" he said.

Right now I'm thinking I might just stay here and look at those lips for a while longer.

"Hey, I'm ready for some of your hot coffee."

His words brought her back to the present, and she felt herself reddening at her thoughts.

"Are you feeling all right?" he asked. "You look a little feverish."

"I'm fine," she lied. In reality, she did feel somewhat warm.

As Gwen pulled through the gate, she felt herself flush even more because Bo had noticed her discomfort. She had to stop having those feelings. *Bo is just a friend. Isn't he? Yes, he's just a friend. A friend who's helping me learn the ropes of ranch life. A friend who just happens to have beautiful blue eyes, tons of muscles, and a very inviting mouth. He is a good friend. Right? Right. He doesn't need you. He seems to be doing quite well without you.*

After Bo had stopped on the porch to feed Pal, giving him an extra helping too, and picking up a few sticks of wood, he came in for his daily coffee.

He opened the stove and shoved the wood inside, removed his gloves, and stood with his hands over the stove. Gwen removed her gloves, stocking cap, and work boots. She was shaking off the coveralls. "I hate winter," she mumbled.

"What?" he turned. "I didn't quite understand that."

"I said"—louder—"I hate winter. Oh, I like to look at the snow from the inside of the house, and I love Christmas, but I don't like having to put on all these clothes to go outside. I hate taking them all off again when I come inside. When I get ready to go outside, I just want to go outside." She waved her arms at the front door.

"Boy, don't get so upset," Bo said. "The way I see it, you have a few options. You can go outside without all those clothes... and freeze. You can stay inside... and your livestock freeze, or you can just go on outside, take the weather, and not complain because there's nothing you can do about it anyway."

"No." She pouted. "I do have another option." She turned toward the kitchen to get his coffee. "I can go back to Dallas where I don't have to worry about the weather...or the livestock." She waited for his reaction. *Am I actually hoping that he will somehow encourage me to stay?* She poured his coffee and brought it to him. Her eyes met his, and Gwen thought she saw a flicker of sadness. *Did I see what I thought I saw?*

"Yeah," he answered, quietly taking the cup from Gwen, his eyes never leaving hers. "There is that one."

Bo drank his coffee quickly. Usually they talked over a couple of cups each morning, but this morning he left early, saying that he needed to get ready to go to town.

As he was leaving, he told Gwen he would just honk as he went by. Suddenly, he seemed more distant, cooler. Gwen stood looking at the door long after Bo had closed it. She felt lonely, as she always did without Bo around. What would she do without Bo? He was all she had. *He is my friend, my helper, and has become, strangely enough, my confidant.*

Gwen walked to the door, opened it, and knew before looking that Pal would be standing there, looking up at her with happy eyes; and he was.

"Come on in," she invited, holding the screen open. "'T'ain't fit weather for man nor beast." Wagging his approval, he padded in and plopped down on the worn braided rug before the stove. "You're my friend too, huh, old man?"

Pal panted a happy answer. "Well, you warm up here for a while. I have to get ready. I have to wait for a *passing honk.*" With that she swept out of the living room.

She was pulling on her boots when she heard Bo's truck coming across the low-water bridge, which was nothing more than a wide span of concrete poured over a creek crossing. She heard two bumps and rattles, one as Bo's truck bounced up on the concrete and one as it landed on the near side.

She stood at the door, waiting for the sound of his horn. Pal was at her knee, waiting to be let out. He heard the truck too and was anxious to meet Bo at the driveway.

"Just a minute," she told him. "I'll let you out after he passes. We mustn't appear too concerned," she added coyly.

Bo's truck proceeded past the old house without a sound. She stood behind the door and wondered if she might have done something to make him angry; maybe he forgot her. She was about to panic when she heard the truck slow to a stop. She pulled her coat from the rack and swung open the door. Pal ran out before her. Bo was backing down the road. He rolled down his window and yelled from the road. "Horn won't honk. Guess it's frozen. I was afraid that you wouldn't hear me go by, so I thought I'd make sure."

"Did you hear that, Pal? He said he was afraid. He was afraid I wouldn't hear. He was afraid I wouldn't know." She squatted down beside Pal and rubbed his head. "Did you hear that, boy?"

She stood and waved a hand at Bo. "Okay!" she yelled back. "I'm on my way."

"I'll just wait here and see if your truck starts. Then I'll be going."

Gwen ran to the pickup and jumped in. As the old thing roared to life, she waved to Bo to let him know. He waved back, rolled up his window, and proceeded slowly down the muddy road. Gwen waved good-bye to Pal and began backing out the driveway. She noticed that Bo was making his way very slowly, just letting his truck idle. Her heart did flip-flops. *He's waiting for me. He's waiting for me*, it sang over and over. Gwen felt warm in spite of the freezing temperature. She followed Bo to town and hoped that he couldn't feel her eyes on the back of his head. She watched his every move and could tell each time he bent to adjust the radio. She flipped the radio on, hoping that they were listening to the same music. When they rolled into town, it was apparent that everyone had the same idea about stocking up. The small town was buzzing with activity.

Moses Fourkiller, the owner of the feed store was standing on the loading dock, beaming as they pulled in. "Well, well," he barked, "our neighbors from the south made it in. What can we do for you?"

Bo alighted from his truck, and even though she couldn't hear what was being said, Gwen could see that Bo was indicating her vehicle and then his. Moses nodded in understanding and waved Gwen around toward the loading dock. She convinced the old truck to go into gear and carefully backed toward the crowded dock. Young Moses, better known as Bubba, was there to tell her when to stop. She could feel the *whump, whump* as each sack of feed was being loaded and heard the truck's springs squeak in protest.

Gwen reached into her alligator bag, which suddenly seemed out of place here at the feed store, and dug around until she found a pen and pad. She would use this time to make a list of things that she needed from the grocery store. As young Moses and another young someone loaded the truck, she sat and made out her list.

"Okay!" young Moses yelled out behind her. She

turned to wave a thank you and was amazed to see the bed of the pickup full of sacks. As Gwen attempted to move forward, the old pickup complained at the amount of weight it was being asked to move. Gwen pressed the accelerator to the floor, and the truck finally moved slowly jerking away from the loading dock so another waiting truck could be loaded.

"I should open a feed store and forget about buying this stuff. This guy's making a bundle," she said under her breath. She reached for her bag, then thinking better of it, reached in and got out her checkbook. She jumped from the truck and hustled onto the dock to pay for what feed she had gotten. As a child Gwen had been in the feed store many times with her father, and she had always felt a little ill at ease in there because she had never seen another female, but today there were two other ladies standing on the dock waiting for tickets. She smiled and nodded to them. They returned her smile. As she reached the top step of the dock, the young someone who had helped load the feed asked her name.

"Collins," she answered. "Gwen Collins." He looked through the tickets until he found the correct one.

"Just take this in the office and give it to the lady at the desk. You'll pay there."

"Thanks." Gwen took the ticket and headed toward the office. She looked down at the paper. The color suddenly drained from her face. She stopped and looked at the ticket again.

"Eleven hundred and fifty dollars!" she whispered. "Eleven hundred and fifty dollars?"

How much feed did Bo buy? There must be some mistake. She turned and looked at the bed of the truck.

That can't be eleven hundred and fifty dollars worth of feed, she thought. *Surely they've made a mistake.*

Deciding that it must be a mistake, Gwen walked into the office and waited until it was her turn to pay. "Hi," she said as she approached the desk. "I was just wondering if this total is correct."

The lady behind the desk took the ticket and smiled up at her. "Yes, Gwen, this is correct." She then laughed. "I'd be wondering, too, if that's all the feed I thought I was gonna get for eleven hundred and fifty dollars," she said, indicating Gwen's truck with her head. "No, that's not all. We're gonna deliver the rest of it tomorrow or next day, weather permitting, depends on how much we've got to deliver. Anyhow, that'll be enough to last until we do get to you." She smiled sweetly.

"Oh," was all that Gwen could manage. She got out her checkbook and scribbled a check. Mentally Gwen was subtracting that amount from her checking account and came up with an amount that was only slightly more than her apartment lease for one month in Dallas. *Yes, definitely, the apartment has to go.* That amount was going to have to last her for the remainder of the winter and no telling how much longer until she had another crop of calves to sell. She handed over the check and in return was handed a receipt. She stuffed the ticket in her pocket and thought about the grocery list. She smiled wryly. She would have to amend that list. At this rate, she wouldn't have enough money to buy groceries. *I'm gonna starve to death this winter while my fat and sassy cows are munching on eleven hundred and fifty dollars worth of feed.*

"Gwen Collins?" She turned to see one of the ladies

who were on the loading dock looking questioningly at her.

"Yes," she answered. "I'm Gwen Collins."

"I'm Joslyn Olsen. Do you remember me?" Without waiting for an answer, she continued. "I was a friend of your mother's. We used to talk for hours on the telephone when you were a little girl. I have a son who went to school with you. His name is George. He was a little older than you."

Gwen screwed up her face and turned her eyes upward in thought. She remembered George Olsen, all right. He wore glasses, braces, and belonged to the academic team. "Yes, of course." Gwen smiled. "I remember George."

"Well, it's really good to see you come home. So many of our young people just can't wait to leave town. It seems they don't want to stay around here after they graduate from high school, and so many of them go away to college and just never return."

"Is George still around?" Gwen asked, pretending interest.

"Yes! George is still here. He went to State, got his degree in business, and now he's a loan officer over at the bank. You should go in and say hello. He would be thrilled to hear from you. They're giving away calendars for next year too. You might need one."

"Yes, ma'am. I'll do that," Gwen said, never intending to. "I may have to talk to him about a loan after buying feed. I never realized how much money it took to feed cows."

"My goodness, Gwen. Are you out there on that ranch? I just figured you'd sell out as soon as I heard about Will's passing. I was real sorry to hear about him dying. Most of the young ones do, you know; sell out, I mean."

"I've heard that about all these young folks." Gwen emphasized *young*. "But I have good help. Bo Bohanan, my neighbor, comes over and helps me do most of my chores. I appreciate him very much."

Mrs. Olsen looked around furtively. "I just don't think I'd trust him. You know he's not from around here. Just comes breezin' in here awhile back and bought that place over there by you. No one'd ever heard of him. I just don't trust people like that."

"I'll be real careful." She looked past Mrs. Olsen and saw Bo coming out the front door of the feed store's office. Gwen threw him a smile.

Mrs. Olsen turned to see the recipient of the smile and immediately turned back to Gwen, scowling. "Remember what I said...be careful." She wagged a finger. Gwen nodded in mock understanding, turning down the corners of her mouth as if to say that it would be their little secret.

Mrs. Olsen turned and walked back toward the office. She couldn't help but meet Bo, who was walking out of the office. "Good mornin,' Mrs. Olsen," Bo said as he passed, and Gwen noticed that he tipped his old battered felt hat. As he neared Gwen, she flashed her most winning smile and, spinning on her heel, put her arm through his so that he could escort her to the waiting truck. The last vision of Mrs. Olsen that Gwen had was a scowl peering out the front window of the feed-store office. Gwen knew she was being naughty, but it felt so good.

"What was that all about?" asked Bo.

"Oh nothing, just girl talk. She's trying to fix me up with her son. Hey, didn't you promise me some chili?"

"I sure did. Are you about ready? I can see that you are by the color of your nose. When the nose turns red, it is a sure indication that you're ready for—trying to fix you up with her son? What, you mean George?" Gwen ignored his question.

"Bo, is there a real need for me to take my truck too? Couldn't you and I just ride together in your truck, and leave mine sitting here until we've finished?"

"George Olsen, from over at the bank?"

"You're changing the subject. May I leave my truck here until we finish?"

"Sure, if that's what you want to do. But now wait a minute, George has a better truck than I do. Want me to call him?" He had that look in his eye again, magically transforming him into a mischievous nine-year-old.

"Stop it. I want to ride in your old, beat up, run down..." She smiled up at him. She suddenly realized that they were flirting with each other... or were they? Was Bo really scared that George Olsen might be a threat? No; and anyway, what difference did it make to either of them?

Gwen was hoping that Mrs. Olsen was still watching. She slid in on the driver's side of Bo's truck, and as they pulled away from the feed store, Gwen pretended there was something in the seat on the passenger's side. She kept brushing an imaginary something out of the seat as Bo got in the truck, so for just long enough, she hoped, Bo and she were sitting next to each other.

CHAPTER THIRTEEN

Christmas was fast approaching, and Gwen had sent her regrets to T. J. She begged off because of weather and the amount of work she had to do. She wasn't making an excuse. The weather was truly horrible, and she did have too much to do to be going off to Dallas. Even after Bo assured her that if she wanted to go he would be happy to do the feeding for her, Gwen still didn't feel right about leaving all the work for him to do, and, besides, she didn't really want to go anyway.

T. J. called her the evening after she received the card from Gwen. After the two of them had chatted for a while, T. J. drawled, "Darlin,' I know how much you have to do on that ranch, so don't make apologies. And if I had a neighbor like you do, that came over every evenin' to help me feed those cows and could cook as well as Bo does and looks as good as he does, Honey, I'd be stayin' close to the fire too. Don't you worry. I just hope you have a wonderful Christmas and don't forget the reason for the season. He's watchin' you, you know. He's takin' care of everything. Maybe we'll see you in the spring. Well, maybe I'll see you in the spring. Next time, I'm comin' by myself. Love you, Gwennie. Bye."

"I love you too, T. J., and I appreciate your understanding. I'll talk to you later and have a lot of fun on New Year's Eve."

Gwen felt a twinge of regret, thinking about the big blow out that her company had on New Year's Eve, but only for a moment. *I have too much to do to think about that.*

Gwen had begun to look forward to Bo's daily visits for coffee but still wasn't in favor of doing the chores with an eight-inch snowfall on the ground. Even though she had been born and raised in Oklahoma, she still couldn't like the extremes in the weather. It was either extremely cold, extremely hot, extremely dry, or extremely wet. *Oh well, regardless of the weather, I don't mind as long as I'm with Bo, and that's beginning to worry me.*

She was thinking about that point when she heard Bo coming across the low-water slab. When she heard the ice crunching under his tires, she cringed. Although she dreaded leaving the coziness of the fire, she rose reluctantly, pulled her coveralls from the coat rack, breathed a deep sigh and began pulling them on. She heard Pal barking from the porch in anticipation. "Keep your fur coat on, dog. I'm coming." Gwen opened the door and was met by a blast of icy air.

She knew before reaching the gate that Bo would give her the weather report. She had never in her life seen anyone who was so interested in the weather. After all, he was the one who said you couldn't do anything about it. "Hey, Dallas!" he shouted, "It's five degrees! Can you believe it? Five degrees! This is just December, and it's five degrees. What's it going to do when winter gets here?"

Placing her free hand on her hip, she said, "And a good morning to you too, Bo."

"Hey, what's the matter with you? You act like you got a letter from Santy Clause that said he had decided to cancel Christmas. Why are you so down in the mouth?"

By this time, Bo had driven through the gate, and Gwen was securing the latch. She galloped to the truck and got in on the passenger's side. "I guess I'm just kinda out of sorts. I miss my family during Christmas. This will be my first Christmas without *any* family. It's kind of lonely. You know?"

"Yes, I know. I told you that if you wanted to go to Dallas I'd stay here and mind your stock. I mean it. If you want to go spend some time with your friends, I don't mind a bit staying here and keeping things going for you. Not at all." Gwen knew that Bo meant it.

"I couldn't go even if I wanted to. The weather is too bad, and besides that, I don't have an automobile that would get me to Dallas." Gwen was making more excuses. She knew that she could hop on a bus and be in Dallas in a matter of hours.

"You said, 'even if I wanted to.' Does that mean you really don't want to?"

Gwen thought about his question for a moment and was startled to realize that she wanted to stay right where she was for Christmas. She looked at Bo with this realization on her face. "No, I really *don't* want to. I'm still not over the way they left here on

Thanksgiving. Every time I look at Pal, I get mad all over again. I know Lance did something horrible to him. I don't think Kaycee would get that close to him, and I know T. J. loves animals."

"What about how they treated me?" Bo complained and puckered his lips.

"You're a big boy. You can take care of yourself. Pal, on the other hand, is just too sweet to be treated badly."

"And I'm not?" He looked at Gwen with a crushed look on his face.

Gwen didn't have an opportunity to answer because they were in the barn, and they got out to load the hay. "Well anyway, I'll be your family, and you can be mine. We'll spend Christmas together. I don't have family to spend Christmas with either, so we will just borrow each other."

Gwen smiled in answer. That was just what she was hoping he would say. She felt bubbles of happiness replacing the gloom she had felt before. She couldn't hug this man, so instead, she just stood beside the truck, grinning and rubbing Pal behind his ears.

The two of them continued with the morning chores, and Bo was excitedly planning what they would do for "their" Christmas. They would have it over at his house. After all, they had Thanksgiving at Gwen's. He was talking so fast that Gwen could hardly understand what he was talking about. She watched and wondered at the energy that he could produce and how quickly time passed when she just sat and listened to this full-grown man who was so animated about Christmas.

When they had finished the feeding and retreated to the house for coffee, Bo was still planning. He had everything right down to the tree. He told Gwen that he would go that afternoon and cut one, and he knew just where to find one. Gwen laughed as she was caught up in his enthusiasm. He raved about a tree he had been watching for a while. The whole time he was talking about going to cut the tree that afternoon, Gwen was devising her own plan on how she could manage a trip to town without him. She would wait until he left, and then she would go get a gift for him. She loved playing Santa, and it seemed that this would turn out to be a good Christmas after all. Gwen knew just what she wanted to get Bo. The two of them had seen it at Kekso's Department Store about two months ago, and at the time she hadn't even thought about buying it for him for Christmas. She began to get anxious for him to leave. The sun had come up well over the mountain, and the warmth would melt some of the snow off the road. Maybe not all of it, but enough so that Gwen was sure she could get to town and back without any trouble.

It seemed to Gwen that Bo had decided to stay all day, but soon he rose, and even though he was still talking about Christmas, he left for home. Quickly, she showered and dressed to go to town. She was afraid that the truck wouldn't start. It was still very cold, and the old thing hadn't been started in a week or so.

Gwen bundled up, and checking to be sure that the stove had enough wood to last until she got back home, she made her way to the truck.

She pulled the key from her purse and turned it in the ignition. The truck sputtered to life. "They don't make 'em like they used to," she muttered and backed down the drive on her secret mission.

The snow had partially melted, as she had hoped, and now instead of snow and ice on the road, she had to deal with mud; but she made it to town with no problem and went straight to Kekso's Dry Goods. She and Bo had been in there a couple of times together, and she hoped that Mr. Kekso remembered one time in particular.

"Gwen, how you been lately?" Mr. Kekso was as bright and cheerful as the sprig of mistletoe he had tucked over one ear. A few sparse strands of silver hair stood out from his nearly bald head. His glasses were forever suspended between the bridge of his nose and the floor, and as he spoke, he peered over the top. "I haven't seen you in a while. I thought that maybe you might have decided to go back to Dallas for the holidays. But, well, I guess when you're the owner of a ranch … well, you know, you are one … all that work." He rubbed his dry hands together in anticipation of a sale. "What can I do for you, Gwen?"

"Mr. Kekso, do you remember a few months ago when Bo Bohanan and I came in here, and I bought some clothes for myself?" She never imagined he would remember.

"Sure, I do. You needed some work clothes. Sure, I remember."

"Right." Gwen was astounded. "Well, anyway. At the time, do you remember a certain felt hat that Bo was looking at? A black one?"

"Let me see." He rubbed his whiskered chin in reflection. "Yes, seems like I do remember. Going to get a little something for him for Christmas?" Mr. Kekso had started walking away. Turning, he motioned for her to follow him back through his over-crowded store through aisles that anyone else would have needed a map to navigate.

Momentarily, his round little body came to an abrupt halt. He looked up. Gwen followed his eyes to an enormous stack of hatboxes. She would never be able to remember which hat it was. She only remembered that it was black and that wasn't much to go on when faced with the prospect of looking through a few hundred hats, probably all black. She didn't even know what size to look for.

Mr. Kekso reached for a long wooden rod with a hook screwed into one end of it. He deftly reached above his head, placed the end of the hook under the top of the box, and pulled, gently at first, then very fast. The individual box flipped out of the stack and was hanging from the end of the long pole. Gwen was amazed and wondered if this device had been an invention of Mr. Kekso's. He opened the box for her.

"This is it, all right." Mr. Kekso grinned. I remember because he looked so handsome in it." The old man lifted it out of the box, and it did seem to be the same hat. Gwen remembered how handsome Bo had looked in the hat too, but she didn't say so.

"This is very nice." She rubbed her fingers across the knap of the hat. It was soft but rigid at the same time. She had no idea how to judge the quality of a hat and was trusting Mr. Kekso to be truthful with her.

"That's one of the best made. Bo would be real proud to wear one like that."

Gwen snuck a look at the price tag on the box. *For that much money, anyone would be proud to wear this hat.* She deducted the price of the hat from the small amount of money she had left and stopped to think it over. She knew she had no more money coming in and would be desperate if she had to buy another batch of feed. "I don't know, Mr. Kekso." She stood thinking when she heard the bell on the front door ringing, announcing another customer. "Why don't you go wait on your other customer, while I think about this for a minute."

"Fine. You just think and look around some more if you like." He squeezed his ample body by her and began his journey back down the narrow winding path between the clothes.

"Hi, Mr. Kekso. What's up? I see you're ready for a Christmas kiss. All decorated up with that mistletoe." Gwen heard the familiar breathy voice. "I have to do some shoppin,' you know. Gotta keep all my men happy... well, one of them anyhow. I don't know what to get for that particular one. What would you recommend?" Francine stood eyeing various things in the store while talking to Mr. Kekso.

"I suppose you're talking about that one from across the mountain." Gwen immediately knew whom they were talking about—Bo. She edged a little closer. She was standing just behind a lofty pile of blue jeans. Francine admitted that was the one that she meant. "Let me see, jeans, shirts..." Mr. Kekso continued. "Socks, boots..." Gwen noticed that he was mentioning everything but a hat. "Just how personal do you want to get, and how much do you want to spend?"

"Well, he's been kinda cool here lately. I'd like to get his head back on track, if you know what I mean." Francine's tone was a little sad.

"If I were you, and I wanted to let him know I cared, this is what I'd do..." Mr. Kekso's voice dropped to a mumble, and Gwen could no longer hear what either of them was saying.

Presently, Gwen heard the bell on the front door and looked up to see Francine flouncing through the door and saw Mr. Kekso making his way back toward her. She quietly moved back to where she was standing before he left. "Okay, Gwen, have you decided?"

She looked at Mr. Kekso, looked down at the hat, looked at the front door of the store, and only hesitated one second before she said, "Yes, I would like to take the hat; but if it's not the one that he wanted or the wrong size, may I bring it back?"

"Surely, surely. You know my motto, or you should by now." She told him that indeed she did remember his very original motto: "satisfaction guaranteed."

The two threaded their way back to the front of the store, where Mr. Kekso proceeded to carefully wrap the gift. "Bo will just love this. I knew he wanted it when he came in here and tried it on, but I also know he has to be careful about spending his money. I guess you do too, though." Gwen nodded agreement. "Bo's a good fellow, but you know how people are around here. I don't know if he'll ever be fully accepted. They just don't trust people who weren't born and raised around here. When Bo first came into town, everybody resented the fact that he bought up one of *our* places without ever living around here, you know. He bought the Janway place sight unseen. Sight unseen! I've always like Bo, though. He never gave me reason to feel otherwise." He continued to wrap while talking. Gwen thought maybe this was the opportunity to ask some questions about Bo.

"What do you know about Bo, Mr. Kekso?"

DONNA BARNARD

Mr. Kekso slowly wagged his head. "I believe," he rubbed his chin, "that he came in here from California. He's been here about five or six years, and one of the main reasons the town didn't take a shine to him was the fact that he came flying in here with lots of money. I heard he paid cash for that place, the Janway place, you know. Spent money like there was no tomorrow. I think it sort of scared people, you know. Most everyone around here just lives from paycheck to paycheck; but he had a bunch of money, and he was spending it. He's kinda cooled down now. Don't spend money like that anymore. Maybe he ran out, but that's just about all I know about him except that I'd much rather see him involved with a really nice neighbor lady of his than a certain waitress. I think she's had her claws out for him ever since he showed up here in town, but Bo can't see her for dust. I've heard that she just can't keep her hands off him when he goes into the restaurant, you know. And I know one more thing about him."

"What's that?" Gwen's interest was suddenly piqued.

"He's gonna get a really nice Christmas gift." Mr. Kekso patted the top of the box as he pushed the beautifully wrapped gift across the counter to her. She paid him what she owed and started to leave. At the door, she turned back. "If I have anything to say about it, a certain waitress might as well start looking somewhere else for her something to sink those claws into, because this neighbor lady has some claws too."

Mr. Kekso whooped loudly and slapped his hands on the counter. "Good luck to you, Gwen; good luck and have a Merry Christmas."

CHAPTER FOURTEEN

Gwen stopped by the grocery store and picked up a few things she needed. She then ran over a mental list that she had planned to get for Christmas dinner and decided that she had accomplished all that she had intended and started home. When she pulled into the driveway, she looked down at her watch. She still had plenty of time to put her things away before Bo came over to help with the chores.

She was just putting Bo's hat in her mom and dad's bedroom closet when she heard Bo pulling into the driveway. "Oh no!" She spoke aloud. "If he sees me with these clothes on, he's going to know that I've been to town." She tore into the living room and grabbed her coveralls to pull on over her clothes.

She was pulling her hair out of the collar when she heard Bo knock. "Hey, you must have been reading my mind. I was going to come over a little early and feed, and then, if you like, we can go into town and get some supper. Huh? How 'bout it?

Gwen threw him a smile. "Sure, I'd love to. I hadn't really been thinking about what to fix for supper anyway."

Gwen pulled on her gloves and yanked her toboggan down over her ears as they began the evening routine of feeding and caring for cattle. Bo was careful to check each of the cows and see that each was doing well for a mother-to-be. Gwen wouldn't have known the difference, but he gave her a lesson each evening on symptoms to watch for if there was going to be any trouble. He also told her that he was going to bring Apple back home. She was, after all, Gwen's horse. She wasn't due to have the foal for another four months or so, and it would give Apple and Gwen an opportunity to become better acquainted.

After the haying was done, Gwen ran back into the house, and Bo left for home. She pulled off her work boots, the coveralls and dropped into the old rocker. She settled comfortably and watched a spider up in one corner of the living room. She imagined her preparing for Christmas by building a new web and putting up a tiny tree. *What do spiders do about cobwebs when they clean house?* she wondered. "I sure hope you're not expecting company for the holidays," she said aloud. She watched for several minutes as the spider wove her web, back and forth, back and forth.

Gwen heard Bo's truck clattering down the road. Quickly, she jumped up, ran into the bathroom, and ran a brush through her hair. "That will have to do," she said to her image in the mirror. As she was putting on her coat, she looked up at the spider's web. "You made me late. Your house is coming down...after Christmas."

She heard Bo's knock at the door as she was pulling on her second dress boot. She yelled for him to come in, but he only stuck his head in. "I'll wait out here, just hurry."

What's his hurry? But when she pulled on her boot and made her way to the door she saw what his hurry was. Beautiful snowflakes were coming fast, and they were large, very large. "Oh, Bo, isn't this pretty? We're going to have a white Christmas!" She turned to look at him. He had a whimsical crooked smile on his face. Puzzled, she asked, "What?"

Still smiling, he said, "Nothing, let's go. I want to get out here and drive in this stuff." He placed his arm protectively across her shoulders. "You ready?"

"Yes." Gwen felt a familiar warmth crawl through her body, all the way from her shoulders down to her toes, which were quickly being covered by the falling snow.

The ride into town was a delight with the snow creating a winter wonderland out of the barren browns and golds of winter. Bo seemed to be an expert at driving on the slick stuff, and they drove to town without mishap. They talked about their plans for a Christmas Eve celebration, and Bo kept a running oratory on what Christmas supper was going to be like. He was making Gwen's mouth water, and she realized she really was hungry and was glad for an invitation to supper. "We're going to have baked ham, candied yams, a green salad, and I've made some candy for us to enjoy along with the rest of it. It's not Christmas without candy. And it has to be homemade. I have eggnog, and for dessert, how about some pumpkin pie? 'Cause it's just not Christmas without pumpkin pie. Is it the same with you? I have to have some pumpkin pie … and what did you get me for Christmas?"

The question came so suddenly that for a second, Gwen was taken aback but quickly regained her thoughts. "You stinker," she scolded, "I'm not going to tell you what I got you for Christmas, *if* I got you something."

"Ah ha, so you did get me something. I saw that look."

"Well, of course I did, but I'll never tell."

"Can I wear it?"

"I'll never tell."

"Is it something I can use on the ranch?"

"I'm not talking."

"Is it bigger than a breadbox?"

She ignored the last question. They were pulling into the restaurant parking lot … the same restaurant where Francine worked. Gwen wrinkled her nose in displeasure.

Bo noticed. "What's the matter? Did you not want to come here?"

"No, this is fine," she lied.

"Well," he said, opening the door, "it better be all right. 'Cause it looks like this is the only thing that's open. I guess everyone was afraid they'd get snowed in, so they all closed up early and went home." He dropped lightly out of the truck, and Gwen slid across to get out behind him.

The restaurant was packed. Gwen supposed all diners had the same idea as she and Bo did. If they were going to have to prepare a big Christmas dinner, why not go out and enjoy a meal prepared and served by someone else? Gwen noticed that, for once, many of the customers were husbands and wives.

They had been seated comfortably when Gwen saw that Francine was indeed working. She was talking to another waitress, and both of them turned and looked in their direction. Gwen knew they had seated themselves at a table that was not one of Francine's tables, and she wanted to do some trading. The other waitress nodded her head. Francine mouthed a "thank you" and began making her way to their table. "Hi, Bo," she whispered breathily. "I've been hoping you'd come in here before Christmas. I have a little something for you. I'll give it to you before you leave." She was talking to Bo, but her eyes were riveted on Gwen. Gwen only smiled her best smile. Mentally, she thanked Mr. Kekso for suggesting something else to Francine besides a hat.

"Aw, Francine, you shouldn't have done that."

"My pleasure, Bo. Anything to *satisfy* you." She threw a look toward Gwen that indicated she could do just that. Gwen just smiled and gave her a look that she hoped would say, "He's sitting with me, Peaches, not you." But she was afraid she only looked silly.

The hamburgers arrived with all the flourish that Francine could muster, and this time Gwen found that she could eat all of the huge burger with no problem. Francine worried around their table like a fly after honey. She made too many trips filling Bo's cup with coffee each time he took so much as a sip from it, and Gwen had completely emptied hers and had to wash down the last of her burger with tepid water. When they were ready to go, Bo rose. Francine bumped over to the table with a rather small box in her hand. "Here you go, *Sweetie.* This is for you." She handed the smaller-than-a-breadbox package to Bo, which was, Gwen had to admit, wrapped beautifully.

"Gosh, Francine, you shouldn't have done this." All eyes were turned toward the three of them, and Bo was turning redder than usual. "I didn't get you anything."

"That's quite all right, *Sweetie.* That's what Christmas is all about... giving. And I love to give. And besides, you've done *a lot* for me." She turned and gave Gwen a "don't you wish you knew what all?" look. "I just wanted to give you something to show how much I appreciate it. I'll see you soon, and *you* have a nice Christmas."

"Well, thanks," Bo said looking down at the gift. "You have a nice Christmas too." He reached down to help Gwen to her feet.

Gwen suddenly felt sorry for Francine. She was trying so hard. And Mr. Kekso had said it... Bo couldn't see her for dust. Feeling the benevolence of the season, she added, "Yes, Francine. I want to wish you a Merry Christmas too." She smiled and patted Francine on the arm. Francine gave her a confused look.

Bo paid their bill, and waving a good night to everyone, they left the restaurant. The snow had piled up in drifts outside, and the cold was invigorating. "Oh, this is wonderful," Gwen said through the fog produced by her words. "Can we walk around the block? I just love to walk in snow."

"Lady," Bo spoke through his own fog, "you're nuts; but if you want to walk in this mess, let's walk." He held out his arm to her, and they walked away from the restaurant arm in arm.

The lights of the small town proclaimed Christmas

everywhere. The cold was biting, but to Gwen it felt good. Everything looked and smelled so clean. They did some window-shopping, and when Gwen saw a package in a window that resembled the package that Francine had given Bo, it reminded her of the present. "Why don't you open Francine's gift?"

"Now?"

"Sure, why not?"

"But it's not Christmas," he argued.

"Okay," she answered. "Don't open it. I know that you probably don't want me to see what your 'girlfriend' bought you."

Bo screwed up his face. "First, she's not my girlfriend. I don't have one of those things. I do have some women who are friends, though; really close friends, if you know what I mean." He grinned meaningfully.

"Yeah, right. I've seen them sneaking over to your place in the middle of the night."

"Ah so you've been watching?"

Are we flirting again? I've got to stop this right now. "Are you gonna open the present?"

Bo reached into his pocket and pulled the small box out and held it to his ear. "Well, it's not ticking." Gwen knew that. He shook it. "Hmmm, it does make some sort of noise."

"Well, open it." Gwen was growing exasperated.

"Really, I would rather wait until Christmas, okay?" He put it back in his pocket. "Why? Are you afraid that you may have gotten me the same thing?" he teased.

"No, I'm not afraid of that. I would just like to see what she got you; that's all."

"Well, you can when you come over for Christmas at the house. I am really looking forward to that." Gwen was too. She slipped her arm back through his, and they continued to walk through the snow. They talked about the beautiful lights, the cold, Christmas dinner, and the cold. Gwen noticed that the wind was picking up making the temperature seem colder. She shivered, and they picked up the pace so they could get back to the pickup. Bo let the truck run to defrost some of the snow from the windshield. "If you need anything, you had better speak now. If this snow continues and the temperature keeps dropping, we will be in for a while; so while we're in town, you had better get what you need."

Gwen thought for a minute. "No,"—thinking about her clandestine trip to town—"I don't think I need a thing."

"So, you do have my gift already." He smiled roguishly.

"You're good." Gwen smiled. He looked like the cat that had eaten the canary.

On the ride home, they continued making plans for their Christmas dinner. Gwen told Bo that she would make a pecan pie and some hot rolls.

"You're actually gonna do some cooking! I can't believe it. I am gonna have to see this."

"My mom did teach me a little about cooking, you know."

When they pulled into the driveway of Gwen's house and Pal had made everyone welcome, Gwen invited Bo in for some hot chocolate. He accepted the invitation with enthusiasm. Gwen allowed Pal in the house to warm himself by the huffer puffer, as Gwen had nicknamed the wood stove. Bo talked to him and rubbed his head, while Gwen made the chocolate. She heard him say something about Santa coming to see Pal because he had been such a good boy. She smiled and was glad that she had actually remembered Pal. She had bought him a new collar and some rawhide bones.

Gwen walked into the living room with a tray laden with chocolate and cookies. Bo looked up and smiled at her, and Gwen felt her heart lurch. "Did you remember to get this dog something for Christmas?"

"Well, of course I did," she answered as she deposited the tray on the coffee table.

Bo looked up at her in disbelief. "You did, really?"

"Yes, I got him a c-o-l-l-a-r and some rawhide b-o-n-e-s."

Bo laughed. "Why are you spelling it? Do you think that maybe he would understand what you were saying?"

She looked down at Pal, who was wagging his stump and smiling up at her. "You never know about this dog. Look at him. I think he's thanking me already."

"I don't believe that, but I do think that he would sure like to have one of those cookies."

She held out one of the cookies to him, and he quickly grabbed it and, dropping cookie crumbs all over the floor, devoured it. He immediately dropped his bottom to the floor and began wagging and smiling again. "No," she said playfully. "You're gonna get fat, and then how will I put the feed out if I don't have you to help me?" When she said the word *no*, Pal stopped grinning at her, and Gwen felt like a heel. "Okay, just one more. Then you have to quit begging. I can't resist those eyes."

She handed him another cookie, and he swallowed

DONNA BARNARD

it without chewing. He went to the rug that lay before the old stove and, making several circles, dropped down. "See, I think he does understand me." She turned to look at Bo, who was looking at her with the same sad-eyed look as Pal had.

"Would it help if I wagged my tail?" he asked, laughing.

Gwen handed the plate of cookies over to him, and he took a handful. They laughed and talked over more chocolate, and the evening went quickly. Bo yawned and looked at the clock. "I guess I had better go. It's later than I thought." He rose and walked to the coat rack at the front door and pulled on his coat. Gwen rose to see him out as Pal padded softly beside her.

"I really enjoyed myself tonight," he said. "I like talking to you." Bo placed his old worn hat on his head. Gwen thought of the new one safely hiding in the closet. He grinned that crooked, heart-melting smile.

"I did too, Bo. It's nice to just sit and talk." Gwen was amazed at how comfortable she felt with Bo. It was as if they had been friends for a lifetime.

He pulled the door open, and Pal shoved his way out. "I'll see you in the morning, if I can get down the road. Look out here."

He held the door open wider. The snow had piled up against the porch and had blown across it so that the porch seemed to have disappeared entirely.

Gwen gasped and, folding her arms across her chest, shivered. "Oh dear," she exclaimed. "This is worse than I can ever remember, but that's okay. Isn't it beautiful?"

"Yes," Bo answered, his look softening as he looked at her, "beautiful." He cleared his throat. "Yeah, it's pretty bad. But," he added, raising his collar, "I'll make it. I'll be here in the morning; and you can just go home with me then, and you won't have to drive over in it. How's that sound?" Gwen stepped farther back into the house. "I don't know. We'll just see how it is tomorrow. Okay? You know I have cooking to do, and that takes time."

"Okay," he answered. "Well, good night." He started out the door. He turned back to face her and looked deep into her eyes. Bo slowly moved his hand to her chin and, cupping it, lowered his head. Gwen realized that Bo was going to kiss her. She was scared, but just for an instant. Her heart told her that this was going to be great. Wasn't it, after all, what she had been waiting for? Finally she was going to get what she wanted. Or was it? That little red sports car came zooming through her mind. *Oh well,* she thought, *it's just one kiss!* She drew in her breath in anticipation and closed her eyes. Bo's lips touched her own trembling ones, and she felt herself drifting as his hand went to her back and drew her in closer. She was sorry that he had on a heavy coat. *I want to feel his body next to mine.* She lifted her hand to his cheek and stepped into his embrace. Bo moved back, and as she lowered her head slightly, she saw he was smiling; but this time it wasn't that irresistible smile. It was a wry grin!

"Why didn't you just tell me you wanted a kiss?" he teased. "You didn't have to do that,"—he looked up toward the ceiling—"to get one. I would have just given you one."

Above her head hanging from the doorjamb was a branch of mistletoe.

Gwen gasped. "You did that! You hung that there."

"Yeah, yeah." He laughed, turned and plowed his way through the snow. Raising his hand without turning, he called, "Good night. See you in the morning." Gwen could hear him laughing all the way to the truck.

Gwen stood with the door flung open for several minutes, but she didn't feel the cold. As a matter of fact, she felt warm all over. She knew who hung the mistletoe in her doorway; it wasn't her. She thought of the little red sports car, but still she couldn't wait until tomorrow night to see what would happen. After all it was Christmas Eve, and Bo had told her that he had something for her. She smiled broadly, hugged herself, and relived his kiss. *It was nice, wasn't it? Yes, it was nice. Aw, heck, it was wonderful.* She backed into the house, closed the door, and stumbled to the old rocker. *Something for me? I hope it's what I want to hear. If only he will let me know how he feels. It would make it so much easier for me to decide what to do.* She couldn't stop grinning. She realized that she must look like Pal asking for another cookie. Thinking of Pal, she went to the door, and yelled for him. "Would you like to come in for the night, old man? It's awfully cold out here." He went to the rug in front of the stove and laid down.

Gwen began clearing the cups away and saw that there was one cookie left on the plate. She offered it to Pal. "Merry Christmas, old man. I hope both of us have a good one. I know what I want for Christmas now. I wonder if it's too late to write a letter to Santa." Pal beat a rhythm on the floor with his stubby tail.

Gwen finished clearing and went to bed, hoping she would have a dream that might possibly come true tomorrow.

CHAPTER FIFTEEN

Gwen woke with a start.

She stretched and smiled, remembering the kiss from the evening before. *My goodness it's cold. I know once upon a time I had an electric blanket. I really need to find it.* Pulling the handmade quilts up and snuggling deeper, she wondered how much more snow had accumulated throughout the night. *I may not want to know. Okay, you really need to get up. You need to build up the fire and make coffee and*—Hearing a noise at her bedroom door, she peeked out from under the cover. Pal was grinning up at her. "Oh my goodness. I am so sorry. I forgot about you being in the house. I imagine you need to go out, huh?"

Throwing the cover off, she reached for her robe and slid into her house shoes. "I have to get up anyway, and you gave me the reason I needed. I need to get the hot rolls and the pie started, and I think I might make some fudge. Wouldn't that be good? Come on, boy."

DONNA BARNARD

She shuffled down the hall to the front door with the dog right on her heels.

Upon opening the door, Gwen was shocked to find about two feet of snow had fallen in the night. She stood, transfixed. She had enjoyed many snows as she was growing up, but she couldn't remember ever seeing this much. *Now how am I supposed to get Bo's hat delivered to his house in this? I'm not very good at driving on this stuff.*

Pal whined. Gwen pushed the screen door open and stood back. As soon as the dog passed through, she quickly closed the door against the cold that was creeping in. Silently thanking Bo for bringing in armloads of wood, Gwen quickly began filling the stove. He had said at the time that she might need it later, and this must be the later he was referring to.

Hurrying back to bed and covering even her head, she lay there, waiting until she could feel the warmth begin to slip throughout the house. Finally she stuck her foot out from under the cover and found that the stove was doing its job, and the house was becoming warm. Sliding from bed, she decided she would postpone bathing until the house was a little warmer; she could at least get started on her part of Christmas Eve dinner. She made her way into the kitchen, made coffee, and began preparing the yeast dough for hot rolls. She returned to her bedroom to dress. *I wonder where Bo is. It's time that he was here.* While making the bed, she heard a vehicle coming down the road. It wasn't Bo's truck, though. She peeked out the bedroom window and saw Pal running to meet the vehicle. It was a large tractor slowly chugging its way down the road and the body perched on the tractor was undeniably Bo's.

A shiver totally unrelated to the weather ran down Gwen's spine. She ran to the living room to grab her coveralls and boots as the tractor pulled into the drive. The machine popped and huffed asthmatically, and Gwen was afraid that at any moment it would choke and suffer a horrible death in her driveway.

"Good morning!" He greeted her as she walked out to open the gate. She smiled back but averted her eyes before Bo could detect her embarrassment, remembering last night. She felt, oddly enough, shy about their shared moment. Bo pulled the tractor through the gate, hooked the utility trailer to the tractor and went matter-of-factly to the usual work of feeding the hungry cattle. He didn't seem to remember last night, so she told herself that she would just have to pretend that she didn't remember it either.

They fed the cows, and since Gwen didn't know how to drive Bo's tractor, Bo loaded the six bags of cubes in the back of the truck and let her put out the feed, while he distributed the hay. When at last the job was done, they headed back to the house. Bo steered the tractor through the open gate and unhooked the utility trailer as Gwen pulled the truck into the yard. When Bo shut the engine off, Gwen assumed he was coming in for his usual cup of coffee, but he surprised her as he came around the side of the tractor by sliding a hand around her waist to gave her a mini hug. "Is that coffee hot?" Looking up at him, Gwen could see that his smile was somehow different. More personal.

"Sure." She looked at the snow-covered ground.

"Good." He removed his hand. "I'm going to go

break the ice on the pond so the cattle can get some water; then I'll be ready for something hot." He started walking off to the storage shed behind the house. "I suppose that maul is still in here?" He raised his eyebrows in question. She shrugged her shoulders. Gwen had no idea where the maul was or *what* one was for that matter.

He plowed a path through the snow to the shed, and Gwen heard him from inside. "Yeah, it's here." Then from the door looking back at her, she heard, "Go on in. I'll do this, and then I'll be in too. Make sure that coffee is hot."

Gwen made her way back into the house and watched from the kitchen window as Bo hit the frozen pond repeatedly. *I guess I'm not much of a rancher. I didn't even think about the ponds being frozen!* "Oh, but I'm learning," she said aloud as she turned to the refrigerator.

She thought probably Bo would like more than coffee after she saw a spray of water hit him in the face. She watched as he wiped it away with the sleeve of his coveralls. She knew he would be frozen to the bone when he did come in, so Gwen started breakfast. She had been waiting for an opportunity like this for a while. She watched as he began walking to another pond.

She put some ham in a large skillet, began making biscuits, and ran to the window and saw that he was still breaking ice. The smell of the ham filled the kitchen, and Gwen realized that she was hungry. She set the table with her mom's china and used the silver that her dad had given her mom on their twenty-fifth anniversary. She cracked eggs and scrambled them quickly. She looked back out the window and saw Bo making his way back to the shed. His nose was as red as a clown's, and she could tell from the amount of vapor produced by his breath that he was winded. And why wouldn't he be? She saw what he was carrying in his hand. *Ah-ha, so that's a maul.* He was carrying what appeared to be an axe, but instead of an axe head, attached to the end was a wedge-shaped, apparently very heavy slab of iron. She watched until he had put the maul away and was headed to the door; then she poured a cup of coffee and set it on the table for him.

He came through the back door into the kitchen, bringing a rush of cold air with him. He stopped, looking at the table. "Oh my goodness, something sure smells good. It smells like your mom's biscuits. How did you know I was starving? I didn't have anything this morning because I wanted to get over here. I figured I'd be here for a long time, and I didn't want to waste time eating." He walked through the kitchen into the living room, where he removed his gloves, coveralls, and boots. "Boy, that smells good," she heard him saying from the living room. "I'll bet it tastes even better than it smells." He smiled as he returned to the kitchen, trying to rub feeling back into his hands. He picked up his coffee and cupped it in his fingers.

Gwen placed a plate of ham on the table and returned to the stove to dish up the scrambled eggs. She was making her way back to the table when he intercepted her in midstride. Sliding one hand around her waist, he pulled her to him. He gave her a simple good-morning kiss. "I wanted to do that as soon as I got here, but I was afraid my lips would be too frozen to feel it; and, lady, that's something I want to feel."

She wasn't sure what to say, so she just asked him if he was ready to have breakfast. He released her and headed to the table. "Yes, ma'am. I'm starved."

Gwen, not quite knowing how to react, simply said, "The biscuits are ready to come out of the oven, so I'll just get those."

As they sat down to breakfast, Bo bowed his head. "Thank you, Lord, for this wonderful food, and bless the one who prepared it. Amen."

Gwen watched as Bo wolfed his food down. After his appetite was sated, he stood, rubbed his stomach, and announced, "I am stuffed. These biscuits tasted just like your mom's. I thought you told me you couldn't cook."

" No, I told you I wasn't *much* of a cook, not that I couldn't cook. I don't *like* to cook, although I do know how."

"Well, you certainly can make biscuits, and you can make my breakfast just anytime you feel the urge."

"It used to be a tradition here at the house. Mom would make a big breakfast on Christmas morning, and we would have breakfast before we opened gifts."

"Well, it's a tasty tradition. Does that mean that you're gonna fix the same thing tomorrow morning?" he asked hopefully.

"I guess you'll just have to wait 'til tomorrow and find out."

Bo rose from the table and added, "Since I had to bring the tractor this morning, I'll go back and get the pickup and come back to get you later."

Gwen thought about her plan to surprise him with the hat. "That's not necessary. I'll drive myself over later. I can probably make it. You've plowed out ruts for me to drive in, and the way that sun is shining, maybe I won't have any trouble anyway. I think it's going to melt some by the time I get ready to come over. By the way, what time do you want me to come over?" Gwen, realizing she was rambling, rose from the table and started clearing things away.

"You can come over any time you want to, but I will have our dinner ready no earlier than seven or eight o'clock tonight. Were you not coming over until it's time to eat?"

"No, of course not. I was going to come over and help you cook. I just didn't know what time you wanted me to come over."

Bo raised one eyebrow in what was supposed to be a seductive look. "Dallas, you can come over and spend the whole day if you want to."

She chuckled. "No thanks. I have lots of things to do around here. I have to clean the kitchen and—"

"And wrap my present."

She gave him a smirk. "Well, as small as it is, that shouldn't take long." She gave him a shove toward the door. "Now get out of here and let me do what I have to do."

He reached for his coveralls and gloves, then looking at his socks, added, "I guess I'd better get my boots, huh?"

She laughed. "I guess you had. The snow might let you know in a hurry that you had forgotten to put them on."

He pulled his coveralls on and stuck his gloves in the pockets. Then he pulled his boots on. "Now the cows have plenty of hay for the rest of the day, so I won't be back over here this afternoon to put out more. As a matter of fact, I gave them a little extra for a Christmas present. I won't be back unless you're afraid that you won't be able to drive over."

"I told you that I'd drive over. Now get out of here before I sic the dog on you."

"A lot of good that would do you. I don't believe Pal would do a whole lot of damage to a complete stranger, let alone his one and only friend."

"I ought to hit you, slandering my dog like that! Go! Get!"

"All right, all right. I'm gone. If you change your mind and want me to come over for you, just call me. Bye."

He leaned down and gave her a passing kiss on the cheek. He waved over his head as he trudged back to the tractor. She closed the door soundly behind her and went right to work in the kitchen. She wanted to get the breakfast dishes cleared away so she could finish preparing her part of dinner then have the remainder of the day to rest and get ready for their Christmas Eve meal. She switched on the radio and listened to carols as she began her work.

For weeks Gwen had been planning on wearing her red silk dress for dinner, but now, considering the weather and the depth of the snow, she had changed her mind in favor of red wool slacks and matching blazer. Her white cashmere sweater and matching silk scarf would have to do. She realized that this was not really a "dinner party," not like she was accustomed to at Christmas, but still she wanted to look nice.

She hoped that she wouldn't feel overdressed for the occasion, but if she did, she could always remove the blazer and scarf. Lately her motto was "comfort first." She laid her clothes out and decided against the cashmere and went for a white sweater of unknown origin. She fussed over which shoes to wear and finally decided she would just carry her white suede boots and wear rubber boots. Her jewelry must be simple, so she chose a pair of gold hoop earrings and a plain gold chain. After deciding what she was going to wear, it was still only three o'clock; she thought she might have time to have a long relaxing bath.

Gwen lingered as long as she thought she should in the bath. Finally, she rose from the cooling water. She still had plenty of time, but she wanted everything to be perfect. This was something she had been looking forward to for a long time. Christmas was her favorite time of year, and since she had been afraid she would spend the holiday alone, she was almost giddy with anticipation at the thought of spending it with Bo.

She pulled the drawer out where she kept her makeup and realized that it had been Thanksgiving since she had even bothered to put any on. She usually just dabbed and slapped. She looked carefully at her face. "Not bad," she said to her reflection, "for not having the facials and moisturizers that you're accustomed to." Still, she promised her face that she would get back into the routine for its sake. As a matter of fact, she thought she just might make it a New Year's resolution.

After she was dressed, she checked the effect in

the mirror and was quite satisfied. "If you don't make an impression on him now, you will never make an impression." She dabbed some perfume behind her ears. Even though the perfume was almost a year old, it still smelled better than the barn!

She checked the clock again. It was five forty-five. Time to get serious. Darkness would soon make driving even more difficult. She brought Bo's gift into the living room, pulled on her rubber boots, and plowed her way to the truck. She returned to the house, placed the hot rolls, pecan pie and fudge in a cardboard box, and picked up the truck keys.

She stepped out on the porch and ruffled the hair on Pal's upturned face. "See you later, old man. Tell Santa Clause where I am." She slogged her way back to the truck, crossed her fingers, and turned the key. Unwillingly, it started. "I don't blame you a bit. I'm asking a lot of you tonight," she said to the truck. She backed carefully out of the drive, and much to her surprise, some of the snow had actually melted from the road. She sent a thank you heavenward and proceeded slowly down the road. It was already dark, and for that she was glad. She wanted to sneak Bo's gift in without him seeing it.

As soon as Gwen pulled into the driveway, Roxie ran to meet the truck. "Hey, pretty girl," Gwen crooned. She noticed the beautiful border collie looking hopefully at the back of the truck. "Sorry, girl. He stayed at home tonight." Gwen reached down and patted her on the head. Roxie retreated back to the porch and as Gwen watched her go, she could see Bo standing at the front door wearing a welcoming smile. *So much for surprises!* She picked up the box of food and decided that she would just have to come back to the truck for his gift. Maybe there was hope after all.

"Welcome to my humble abode. " He reached for the box and stood aside for her to enter. "Yum, this smells delicious. And so do you."

She shook out of her coat, removed her gloves, and had just started removing the rubber boots when suddenly it occurred to her that she had forgotten her white suede boots—and here she was with her pant legs rolled up to her knees, wearing the boots she fed cattle in ... and she was trying to make an impression? She moaned.

"What's the matter?"

"Oh, I just realized I forgot my boots ... I mean the boots that I was going to wear after I pulled these off. I left them at home." She indicated the rubber work boots.

"Don't worry. I'll go get them if you will just watch dinner for me." He was pulling on his coat and reaching for his own rubber boots.

"No, no. You don't have to do that ..." Then she thought of the hat sitting in the truck. This was the perfect opportunity. "But if you would like to, I'm sure that I left them sitting right by the door."

"No problem. I'll be back in a jiffy." He leaned down and planted a kiss on her cheek. "Bye. And he was out the door.

Gwen waited until she heard his truck leave the driveway, then pulled on the work boots again. She made her way out to the truck to get his gift. She pulled it from the seat and plowed her way back through the snow to the house. Once inside, she had to take the boots off again and placed them in exactly the same spot, hoping Bo would not notice that they had been moved. "You're becoming paranoid," she told herself.

She took the box to the tree and carefully placed the package toward the back so that Bo wouldn't notice it. She stood back and looked to see if it was too obvious. She decided it wasn't. There were very few gifts under the tree, so she couldn't actually hide it. She studied the tree. Bo had been right; it was beautiful and just right for the two of them. *Oh, my gosh. I'm thinking of us as us!* She opened the candy and placed it on the coffee table.

Only then did Gwen look around the living room. There was a bowl of popcorn sitting on the floor, and a string with the beginnings of a popcorn string for the tree. The smells coming from the kitchen were making Gwen's mouth water. She sneaked toward the kitchen and stuck her head through the door. There were pots on the stove puffing steam, and she noted that the timer was clicking. She walked over and checked it. The needle was sitting on fifteen minutes. *I hope Bo's back by that time, because I have no idea what has only fifteen minutes left to cook.* She lifted a few lids and saw that they were having green beans, one of her favorites, and yams. The oven was on, so she peeked in and raised her eyebrows in surprise. There was a huge lump of brown bread in an enormous pan. She stood looking at it for a moment because she could not figure out what this monolithic loaf of bread was doing in the oven. *I can just see us trying to make sandwiches out of that size of bread!* She chuckled to herself. She closed the oven and strolled back into the living room.

The Christmas tree lights were blinking cheerily, and she just couldn't resist the temptation any longer.

Even though she knew there was no one else in the house except her, she looked around furtively and made her way to the Christmas tree. She knelt down in front of it and immediately saw the gift that Francine had given Bo at the restaurant and sneered at it. At least Gwen was the one having Christmas Eve dinner with him ... not her. Bending a little closer, she noticed her name attached to a rather small gift. She picked it up and shook it, there was no sound. She replaced it just exactly where it had been, again reminding herself that she was truly paranoid. She started to the fireplace when she saw, partially hidden behind the sofa, another gift with her name on it. It was not small. She carefully pulled it from its hiding place and read the tag. "To Dallas. With Love, Bo." *I wonder if it's boots? It looks like a boot box.* She gave the box a shake. "Nope," she said, "it's not boots. Too quiet for that."

She smiled and read the tag again. "With love, huh?" she said aloud. She heard the truck coming down the road, and she hurriedly replaced the box, making sure that it was just exactly as it had been. She gave the present a last look, and nodding in satisfaction, trotted back to the chair in front of the fireplace. With a second thought, she went to the door and opened it so that she could greet him and hoped that the cold would wipe the guilty look from her face. The timer sounded.

Bo's truck bounced down the drive, and under the night light, she saw him smile at her. She returned his smile, hoping that she didn't look too guilty. He lighted from the truck and had her boots in his hand. "I found them exactly where you said they were."

"I heard the timer go off. I didn't know what to take off the heat."

Bo picked up speed and tried, unsuccessfully, to run through the deep snow. He was a funny sight trying to leap over the snowdrifts using only the illumination from the porch light and the night-light. He jumped up on the porch and handed her the boots on his way through the door. "I forgot all about the timer," he said. "That was for the ham in the oven."

"A ham? In the oven?" He handed her the boots, and she followed him into the kitchen and watched as he removed the gigantic loaf of bread. "That's a ham?"

"Sure," he assured her. "The ham's in the bread. It keeps the ham moist, and the bread has a delicious smoky taste to it. Pretty neat, huh?"

Bo began removing the bread from around the ham. After all the bread was removed, he placed the ham on a beautiful Christmas platter. It was resplendent. "It won't be long now. Are you hungry?"

"I'm starved."

"Good." Bo flicked one eyebrow in another attempt at looking seductive. "That's the way I like my women. Keeps 'em humble."

Gwen had to laugh. She swung a glancing blow at his arm, and he danced out of the way. Laughing, he turned to her. "You can help set the table, and since I don't have a dining room, I moved a card table in front of the fireplace if that's all right with you."

"I think it's a wonderful idea."

The meal was delicious. Conversation over dinner was light and mostly about the work he had done on the Janway place since he had bought it. She could see most of what he had done with the house, but when he started talking about the outside work, she found her thoughts drifting to the treasures beneath the tree. Bo knew that he had lost his audience when he asked, "Are you ready for dessert, or would you rather open gifts?"

"What?" The word *gifts* had awakened her.

"Do you want dessert or do you want to open gifts?"

"How do you know that you even have one?" she teased.

"You don't think I really fell for that forgot-my-boots scam, do you? I knew that you just wanted to get me out of the house so you could bring in my gift. I knew." He wagged an accusing finger at her.

She just smiled. She couldn't let him know that she actually had forgotten the boots and that the situation had just worked out perfectly.

"You think you're pretty smart, don't you?"

Bo stood and stretched. "And besides, I saw the box under the tree when I came in." He smirked. "Okay. Here's the deal. I'll get us some coffee and pie, and you get each of us a present. Then we'll eat dessert and open presents. How's that sound?"

"Sounds good to me." Gwen moved toward the Christmas tree. "Wait, we have to have some Christmas music."

"Turn the radio on!" Bo yelled from the kitchen.

She located the power button on his stereo and was greeted by the sounds of Christmas. She reached under the tree and pulled out Francine's gift. She wanted him to open it and get it out of the way. She picked up the small package with her name on it and laid them both on the coffee table. She had started to the kitchen to help Bo, when he appeared at the door with a tray. He had coffee and pumpkin pie that had been piled high with whipped cream. He spied the gifts and grinned impishly when he saw which gift she had laid before his place. He unloaded the tray. "What do you want to do first, eat or open?"

"I don't know. What do you want to do?"

"I'll tell you what. Let's take a bite and then tear a little of the paper. By the time we finish the pie, we should have the gifts open. How's that?"

"Good." She already had a bite on the way to her mouth. She laid her fork down on the plate and tore a tiny bit of the gift wrap off her box.

Bo took a large bite and ripped a large piece of the paper from his gift.

"No fair," Gwen whined. "You tore a bigger piece of paper than I did."

"I took a bigger bite than you did."

She shrugged. "Okay." She dug deeper into the pie and opened wide, but she didn't open wide enough for the whipped cream. She had the white stuff all over her mouth and reached for a napkin. They both laughed.

She finally managed to get the pie down and tore a piece of paper off that she thought would be fair. Bo didn't complain, and she could see why. He was wolfing down his pie and dropping paper all over the floor. She began eating and washing it down, but she knew she couldn't beat him, so she matched him bite for bite. At last they had the boxes unwrapped, and all they needed to do was to open them. He slowly lifted the lid off the gift and peered inside. Gwen was more anxious to see what Francine had gotten Bo than what Bo had gotten her. He slowly lifted his head, and she could see a silly smile spread across his face. He lifted his eyebrows.

"Wow, this is exactly what I wanted for Christmas. This is why I wrote Santa. Francine really knows how to please a guy. Gwen felt her heart sinking. What was it that Bo had wanted?

"What is it?" She tried to sound uninterested.

He held the box out for her to see. Lying in the box, cuddled in a mound of tissue paper, was a smaller box of aftershave. Gwen was puzzled. Bo saw her expression and laughed. "I don't wear aftershave. Never have, never will. I wonder if Francine is trying to tell me something. Maybe I need to wear some, huh?" Gwen felt relief sweep over her, and to her surprise, found she had been holding her breath, waiting for Bo's reaction. She let her breath go, and it sounded much like a sigh. She smiled at Bo and sent another thank you to Mr. Kekso.

"Now, let me see what else I have hidden under the tree." He knelt under the tree and lifted the large box containing the hat. "To Bo. From Gwen," he read.

She knelt down beside him under the tree. "Now do I get to see what's in this box that I unwrapped?" She held up the box containing her gift from Bo.

A look of embarrassment swept over his face. "I'm sorry. I completely forgot. You'll have to forgive me. Christmas brings out the kid in me. Yes, open it. I hope you like it." She took the box and started trying to get through the layers of tape that Bo had used to close the box. She gave him a frustrated look. He just turned his eyes upward and smiled.

Finally, the tape was beginning to come away. By the time all of the tape was off, the box was completely demolished. It looked as if Pal and Roxie had been playing with it. She pried off the top, and as she did so, she looked up at Bo. He had a goofy smile on his face.

Under the lid she found lots of cotton. Deep in the cotton, she found a pin. It was in the shape of a cowboy hat with rhinestones around the edge of the brim. She was disappointed but didn't want to show it. She supposed he wanted her to have the pin for a reason, so she was glad he had chosen it. In the back of her mind, she found herself wondering if Francine had suggested to Bo that he buy this pin for Gwen. She raised her head, hoping that Bo could not read her face. "Thank you, Bo. This is very thoughtful. It's really a very pretty pin." She leaned toward his cheek, and seeing her kiss coming, he leaned into it and planted one on her lips.

"You're welcome. I saw one like that on a lady in the feed store once, and I liked it so much, I figured you would like one too." Gwen took the brooch from the box and started to place it on her sweater, when Bo reached across and took it from her. "Let me do that." He worked the pin through the sweater. "I have to do this just right. I know just how to treat this type of pin. You have to be just where the light will catch it." Bo was working his way closer to her. She could feel the warmth of his body and could smell his manliness. He didn't need aftershave. She liked his scent just the way it was. He secured the pin to her sweater and wrapped his arms around her. "Did I tell you that you look beautiful tonight? These tree lights just add the perfect accent." She could feel her body reacting to his nearness. She wanted to feel the strength of his arms around her. She wanted—"Wait a minute." He pulled away from her. "I almost forgot. I have another present to open, don't I?" He unwound his arm from her and reached for the gift. "How about if I shake it first?" Gwen shook her head.

"No? Well, all right. I'll just tear into it." He looked questioningly to her. She nodded. Bo started tearing paper from the box. He was just like a kid, and she smiled at his enthusiasm. When the paper was off, he held the box up to the light and could immediately see what kind of box it was. His mouth dropped. "Is this really what's in this box?"

Gwen shrugged her shoulders. "Why don't you open it and see for yourself."

Bo lifted the lid and looked inside. She heard a sharp intake of breath. "It is! It really is! I've wanted this hat for a really long time. How did you know?" He looked at her and understanding crossed his face. "Oh, yeah. I remember. You were with me one day when I went into Kekso's and tried it on."

Bo carefully removed the hat from the box and placed it on his head. "How's that?" he asked. "I'll have to have it shaped, but that's nothing. I can do that myself." He was turning, modeling for Gwen. Gwen felt a warm flush over her body. The hat, along with the closeness of Bo, and the season, filled her with a longing that she had not felt in a long time. He leaned down to her and placed a warm, intimate kiss on her lips. She felt her body reacting, and she placed her hands on his cheeks, pulling his face down her hers. He relaxed and pulled her body to his so that they were both kneeling before the Christmas tree, locked in an embrace. He pulled his head back. "Guess what?" He whispered in her ear. The whisper made shivers run up her spine. She sent a silent prayer. *Please let this be what I want for Christmas. Please let him say—*

"What?" she answered, throatier than she wanted or expected.

"I have something else for you."

Gwen thought, *I know what I want,* but said, "Really, something else?" Gwen innocently looked under the tree. "There aren't any more gifts."

"No, not under the tree. You just sit here, and I'll go get it. You have to close your eyes though. Don't open them until I tell you to, okay?"

In answer, Gwen closed her eyes, and lay back on the floor, her hands behind her head. She thought about the boots that she had sent Bo back to her house for. They were still sitting by the front door where Bo had left them. She felt her body slowly relaxing. She could hear Bo's footsteps coming back closer. She closed her eyes tighter. She knew when he walked into the living room and was waiting for him to tell her to open her eyes. She wondered what he could have gotten her that would require so much secrecy. She could feel her curiosity building and could hardly wait to open her eyes. "Now?" she asked.

"Just a second."

She heard the shuffling of feet and other noises but nothing that she could recognize as a gift. No paper shuffling or rattles, just the sound of Bo's feet.

"Now," he said quietly.

She slowly opened her eyes. Before her sat a beautiful, hand-carved wooden rocker made of beautiful maple. She gasped. "Oh, Bo! This is beautiful." She rose and walked over to it and ran her hand over the curved arms and across the back. She stared at Bo who had a self-satisfied look on his face.

"I thought you might like that. I know how you like

to sit in that old rocker of your mother's. Go ahead, try it out."

She sat down and curled her feet up under her the same way she sat in the mother's rocker. She leaned back and closed her eyes before pulling her head forward and beginning to rock. The only thing missing was the familiar squeak. "This is wonderful, Bo. Thank you so much. I couldn't have asked for anything any better, and you couldn't have given me anything that I would prize more than this. I really had no idea that you had bought anything like this."

"I didn't buy it. I made it. I made it for you."

"You made this?" she asked, rubbing her hands over the satin finish. She thought of the barn wood cross and the matching table in Bo's living room that had been made from barn wood and a rifle.

Bo placed his hand on the back of the rocker and rocked her. She leaned back happily and thought better of saying anything more. She shut her eyes and no sooner had she done so than she felt Bo's face once again close to hers. She opened her eyes and found herself looking into those mesmerizing blue eyes ... upside down.

She smiled lazily. As Bo's face began moving closer to hers, she could feel her heart racing. She hoped Bo couldn't hear it. His lips closed over hers, and she felt herself responding. She pulled away from him and rose from the rocker and walked to where Bo was standing. She reached up and placed her arms around his shoulders. She placed one hand on the back of his head and drew his lips to hers. He held her tightly against his body, and his hands played over her back and slowly dropped to her waist. She pulled back from him and out of the corner of her eye saw the light from the rifle lamp softly shining. Its rays illuminated the Bible that lay on the table. *What are you doing? You can't do this.* She pushed back from Bo, ashamed. She took a step back. "I'm sorry," she whispered, not trusting her voice.

Bo took a deep breath and turned away. "No, I'm the one who should apologize. I was entirely out of order." He turned away from her, put his hands on his hips, and stared at the ceiling for what seemed a long time. Then he turned and looked at Gwen with his crooked smile. "I'll help you get your things together." She guessed that this was his way of saying that the evening was over. She walked to the door, rolled up her pants legs, and pulled on the old rubber boots. She bent down to pick up the white boots and smiled. At least they had worked to get Bo out of the house while she had gotten his gift from the truck. She glanced up at Bo, but one look at his face told her that she shouldn't say another word. She could see frustration and hurt on his face, and she didn't want to add anything else.

She pulled on her coat and silently left his house. On the short trip home, she felt under her coat to see if the pin was still in place. It was. She closed her hand around it, and tears began to splash down on her coat.

When she got home, she slipped out of her coat and let it fall to the floor. She walked to piano and looked up at the picture of Christ. She lifted her hand and let her fingers gently trail across the glass. "Father, you have to help me. I don't know what to do. I am so undecided about what to do with the rest of my life. I need him to tell me that he wants me to stay—that I have a future with him. Should I tell him how I feel? What do I do?" The tears that had started on the trip home became heart-rending sobs. She made her way to her bedroom and fell across the bed. Her tears did not stop until she had cried herself to sleep.

The next morning dawned dazzling clear. The reflection of the sun from the snow was blinding. Gwen stood looking out the window. She had always loved the way snow made everything look clean and new. None of the dreariness of winter showed through. Even the naked trees were dressed in a beautiful blanket of snow. The dormant trees of winter were always depressing to her, and now the snow had worked its magic to hide the ugliness that winter always brought. It suddenly occurred to her that today was Christmas. Thoughts of Christmas brought back memories of what had transpired between Bo and her the night before. She felt crimson creeping up her neck and onto her cheeks. She turned from the window and went into the bathroom. The face that looked back at her from the mirror was not hers. It was the face of some ugly, swollen person.

The mascara that she had so carefully applied the evening before had smeared its way down her face and settled into black smudges, which ran across the bridge of her nose and oozed it way to everything below her eyes. The lids of her eyes were hideously swollen and puffy. She felt the tears begin to well up. She banged the bathroom cabinet in anger. "Come off it, Gwen. Gather yourself together and forget what happened last night. You have better things to do than to go mooning around after some hayseed." She took a deep breath to fight the tears she felt threatening and let it out slowly. Grabbing a washcloth, she lathered up and began scrubbing at the dark smear across her face. She pressed down hard on the cloth to wash the mascara off but at the same time recognized she was trying to wash away the memory of last night. She knew if she could stay angry it wouldn't hurt so much. She decided she would blame it all on Bo. *Yeah,* she thought, *I'll blame it all on him. That way I can stay mad. It wasn't my fault. It was his.* Gwen knew, though, that it was her fault too. She shouldn't have led him on. "See what you get?" she said to the mirror. "You should know better."

She rinsed her face in cold water, hoping its iciness would take some of the swelling out of her puffy eyes. After rinsing her face, she dried it with a vengeance and studied the effect in the mirror. Now what she saw was a deep red face with puffy eyes. Well, at least the face was not so horrifying. She dropped the towel and washcloth into the clothes hamper with resignation and dragged herself into the kitchen to start the coffee.

She threw an extra measure in the basket, hoping to make it strong enough to wake her. She knew Bo wouldn't be over this morning to help with the feeding, and she would have to do all of it by herself. She thought maybe that caffeine could help her cope with what she faced. The thought of Bo brought back last night, and she remembered the rocker. *Oh well, it was beautiful, but I guess he needs to give that to someone he can really care for and who will really care for him.* She thought of the pin, and because she had on the same clothes, it was still pinned right where Bo had put it. "Yuk," she said aloud to the kitchen window. "I guess I'd better have a shower." She pulled herself down the hallway and into the bathroom. She stared into the mirror again. "So, you're back," she accused the reflection. "I thought probably you would come back if you ever got your thoughts collected enough to think that you hadn't even undressed last night."

Carefully she removed the pin from the sweater and laid it on the bathroom cabinet. She pulled the sweater over her head and removed her slacks. She dropped her clothes in the hamper, but before climbing in the shower, she gently touched the pin.

The shower felt good and refreshed her spirits somewhat. Today was Christmas, and she should try to do something to celebrate the occasion. As she let the water run rivers down her body, she decided she would call T.J. later in the day and wish her a Merry Christmas. They had hardly talked since Thanksgiving, but because the holidays were always their busiest time of year, she forgave T.J. and the gang for not calling her. Gwen knew that T. J. would keep her job open because she was always true to her word and a shrewd businesswoman. She knew a good thing when she saw it, and Gwen knew she was a good thing. It wouldn't be too long before she would be reckoning with the prospects of selling the house and returning to Dallas. She had already been living back home for almost five months, and only seven more to go. She stepped from the shower and wrapped a towel around her. She could smell the coffee and hurriedly wrapped a towel around her head. She walked barefoot into the kitchen and poured a cup of coffee. She planned on drinking coffee while sitting in her mom's rocker, but when she turned to the old rocker, instead, sitting before the stove was the new rocker, the one that Bo had made her. She

DONNA BARNARD

padded into the living room and gave it a push, which started it rocking. "How in the—" She saw movement from the corner of her eye. She jumped, spilling coffee on the floor. Bo was sitting in the old rocker, which had been moved toward the front of the living room. "How did you get in here?"

"Well, I came through the front door. I knocked, but I suppose from the looks of things, you were in the shower."

It was then that Gwen realized she was standing with only a towel around her.

"Excuse me. I'll be right back. There's coffee." She threw these last words back as she was making her way back to her bedroom.

Once in her room, she threw some clothes on. Then she became angry. *How long has he been here? Did he hear me talking to myself? Oh my goodness. He thinks I'm crazy as it is, but now he's certain.*

She stomped back down the hallway. "Now, how did you get in here?"

Bo smiled at her, but it was an uncertain smile. *Does he actually want to forget what happened last night? If he does, thank you, God. I'm all for that. I'm not really angry; I am ashamed and guilty. That's what I'm feeling, so if he wants to forget it, I'm willing, but I still think the air needs to be cleared.*

"I told you. Through the door. I guess you left it unlocked last night. Honest, I was just going to leave the rocker and the gift and disappear. I really thought you were still asleep. I didn't mean to scare you or upset you. Anyhow, here's another gift. You forgot it last night." He handed Gwen the box that she had seen the night before behind the sofa. She noticed, sadly, that the nametag had been removed.

"You want me to open it now?"

"Well, yeah," he drawled. "It is Christmas, you know."

Gwen slowly removed the paper from the box, fully aware that Bo was watching her every move. Yes, it was a boot box, but inside lay a hand-crocheted afghan done in a zigzag pattern with deep blues, light blues, and white. "Oh my goodness, Bo. This is beautiful. I hate to think that you made this too. I'm still in shock thinking about you making this rocker, but the afghan—"

"Well, wood working is a hobby of mine, and no, I didn't do that," he said, indicating the afghan. There's a lady in town that makes those. I thought it'd be pretty on the rocker."

Gwen shook it out. It was large enough for her to snuggle under. She sat down in the rocker and pulled the afghan up to her chin. "Thank you. This is just too much."

"Well, the only thing you need now is a cup of coffee. Can I refill your cup? You sort of spilled yours."

Gwen handed him her cup. "Thanks. How long have you been here?" She was having trouble knowing how to react to his presence. She was still terribly embarrassed about the night before, felt her cheeks begin to redden.

"Oh, I don't know," he answered. "After I let myself in, I could smell the coffee, so I knew that you were up. That's when I decided to make myself comfortable and wait for you. We still have to feed, you know. Cows don't care if it's Christmas or not. They want to eat every day. I figured you could use the help." Bo

DONNA BARNARD

had risen and was making his way into the kitchen. "That coffee does smell good, and I haven't had any this morning."

She placed her hands on the arms of the rocker and felt the smooth, cool wood. She leaned back, deciding Bo was right. The rocker was perfect for these cold mornings when she sat before the old stove and warmed her feet.

Bo brought the coffee in the living room and held hers out to her without a word. He made his way back to where he had set the old rocker and sat down. From the awkward silence, she guessed that Bo was as uncomfortable as she was with the memory of last night. "Would you like to join me up here by the fire?" Bo silently rose, picked up the rocker with one hand, and moved it closer to the fire. They sat in silence for a time, and she could tell that they were both thinking of what had passed between them the night before.

"About last night..." he started. She could feel a sickening dread rising in her chest. "I'm sorry. I guess I was just going too fast. I shouldn't have read more into our relationship than was there."

"No, I'm the one who should apologize," she added, surprising herself. "I'm guilty of making you feel that way. I'm sorry. I'm ashamed, and I'm humiliated. Our friendship means more to me than that, and I don't want to do anything to jeopardize that friendship."

"Well, okay, we're both sorry. I think we should agree not to bring it up again. What do you say?"

Gwen felt relief wash over her. "I'd say that's a very good idea." She smiled up at him, and he quickly lowered his head to study his cup.

Gwen realized it was going to take more than one day for their relationship to return to its former level.

The feeding went well, and at the end of the work, Gwen felt that she and Bo were in better frames of mind. Bo invited her over for a Christmas lunch of leftovers. "I'll be back early to help put out the hay, then we can go back over to my house to eat. I may even let you warm up some of the leftovers." He smiled, and Gwen saw a shadow of the old familiar boy-like friend. For the first time that Christmas day, she drew a comfortable breath. Although the incident from last night wasn't forgotten, she felt she had been forgiven, and that meant a lot to her.

She hoped that this evening would go better than the previous one, but she had mixed feelings about going back to Bo's house.

DONNA BARNARD

CHAPTER SIXTEEN

Gwen hurried around so that she wouldn't be late for supper. She tried her best to look good for Bo, and the entire time that she was trying to look her best, she was wondering why. She didn't want him to think that she liked him in that way, but still, she wanted to look nice. *I'd want to look nice if I went to town to get groceries, and I don't have a crush on the guy in the meat market. You don't have to overdo it, just be yourself.*

She decided on jeans, a sweater, and a pair of winter socks that matched her sweater. *That way when I take off my rubber boots, I will still be okay.* She didn't put on much makeup and pulled her lengthening hair into a ponytail at the nape of her neck. She pinned her new cowboy hat pin to her sweater. She decided it wasn't so bad after all. She patted it lovingly.

She checked the stove to be certain there was enough wood to last until she returned, noting that there probably wasn't enough, she added more and checked the damper. She began pulling on clothes. *I'll be so glad when I don't have to dress for the Arctic!*

After dressing, she pulled on her coveralls . She pushed the door open, and waiting for her exit was Pal. He was ready to go wherever she wanted to go. He smiled his doggy smile and begged by way of a stubby tail to be allowed to accompany her. She reached down and scratched his head. "Okay, you can go visit Roxie if you promise to behave yourself." She wagged her finger at him as if he were a recalcitrant child; and he promised, or so he appeared by the look of sheer innocence on his face, and they proceeded to the truck.

Gwen decided to try to feed by herself and go over to Bo's house to surprise him. She jumped into the old truck and turned the key. The old machine grumbled but came to life as it always did. She let it warm for a few minutes and proceeded to drive down the driveway that led into the pasture. Pal sat happily in the bed of the truck and let his tongue loll out as far as it would go. Gwen couldn't help but smile at him through the back glass. He was as happy going to the barn as he would have been going to town. Gwen supposed he would be happier going to the barn than to town, for as far as she knew the dog had never been to town. Laughing at the thought of Pal padding down the sidewalk, she backed into the barn and hopped down from the truck, leaving it running to further warm the engine and the cab. She began loading bales of hay and noticed lately they seemed lighter. She supposed she was getting stronger. She grinned to herself. *Me? With muscles?*

After loading the hay, she pulled the truck out of the barn. The cows heard the truck and had begun bawling and gathering in their usual feeding place.

DONNA BARNARD

Gwen was very proud of herself, for what she was doing. She was *doing* for herself! The cold air on her face felt good. The peace and serenity of being alone with the cows and Pal were very special to her. She reveled in the aloneness. She was alone but not lonely. Sometimes when she lived in Dallas, although surrounded by many people, at times she felt lonely.

At first when she moved back to Long Prairie, she had felt miserable without her friends and her social life, but lately she had not felt lonely—not even when she was alone. She reached down and gave Pal a scratch. "I guess it's you, old man. You are *my* kind of people. I'll always have you."

She threw the squares of hay over the truck bed. It was funny to watch the reaction of the cows when they saw it wasn't Bo who was scattering hay. For some of the cows it was business as usual, but a few eyed Gwen as if she had three heads. Gwen giggled at their reactions. "You girls better get over her and get a bite or two, or it's all gonna be gone."

She then went back to the barn to feed and hay Apple. She went into the feed room, scooped up a bucket of feed, and went to the stall door. Apple nickered in recognition. "Hi, girl. How're you doing this evening?" Apple blew hard through her nose. Bo called it "blowin' her rollers." He said horses do that when they are confused or scared. Gwen could tell Apple was upset but had no idea why. "Hey, what's the matter with you?"

Apple quickly spun and went to the open window on the east side of her stall. She looked out the window, pinned her ears flat to her head, and blew hard. Gwen dumped the feed into her feed trough. "What do you see out there? Is it another turkey? I know you don't like those old struttin' gobblers." Gwen laughed and ran her hand under Apples mane and patted her. "It's okay. Let me look." Gwen looked down the pasture through the open window. Through a low hanging mist, she could see nothing that Apple would be upset about. There were only trees, the creek, and snow. She turned back to Apple. "I don't see a thing, girl."

Gwen walked out of the stall, looked through the open double doors, and still saw nothing to the east. She took the wheelbarrow to the hay bales, loaded about half a bale, and pushed it back to the stall. Apple was standing just inside the gate. She was pawing the ground and had begun to sweat. "Back. You're gonna have to back up and let me in there. I'll look again." Gwen tore the squares of hay apart and dumped them in the manger then turned to the window. "Okay, let me look again." Apple was standing, obviously still upset, right beside Gwen. Gwen crooned to her and rubbed her in an effort to calm her down.

"I'm sorry, I don't—oh my gosh!" After an intake of breath Gwen whispered, "Apple, is that what you're so upset about? Oh my gosh!" From behind an ancient oak tree sprang a large red-earth colored panther. It only hit the ground twice before leaping over the barbed wire fence. It cleared the fence with no trouble, landed in the ditch that ran alongside the county road, and bounded up the hill that lay across the road from the pasture.

"I don't blame you for being so upset. That was scary." In a slightly louder tone, Gwen admitted, "But it was really exciting too." Apple calmed down and although she went back to the window a few more times to make absolutely sure that the cat was gone, she dropped her head to the grain and began eating. Gwen remained in the stall with Apple until she had calmed down. "Well, girl. If you will excuse me, it's my turn to eat." She ran her hand lightly over Apple's expanding girth. "You're worried about that baby, huh? I don't blame you. I'll see you in the morning. You have a good night, and if you need me, all you have to do is call." Gwen chuckled. "I can't wait to tell Bo about the panther." Since everything was done in the house, she decided to just drive over to Bo's house.

Pal was happily standing in the bed of the truck with his front feet on the wheel well, letting the cold air blow into his face. His ears were flapping in the breeze, and his tongue was lolling out of this mouth. He looked so happy, Gwen wondered if he knew they were headed to visit Bo and Roxie.

The road was still treacherous in several places because the snow had been packed down to solid ice, and even though she was in a hurry, Gwen drove very carefully.

As she neared Bo's house, she could see him and Roxie in the pasture feeding his own stock. She slowed to a stop. She wanted to memorize the scene. *It looks like a scene you might see on one of those calendars they give out at the feed store.*

Pal barked from the back of the truck, Bo turned and threw a hand up in greeting; Gwen waved back. He smiled one of those million-dollar smiles. Her heart fluttered. "You stop that," she admonished herself and smiled feebly.

She pulled the truck into the drive-through gate

and got out. She started walking toward Bo, and Pal jumped down out of the truck and ran to greet Roxie.

"I thought you were going to wait for me to come help you with the chores. Is there something wrong?"

"No," she answered. "I've already finished the chores, and so I thought I would come over here and help you with yours." This she said with more than a little pride.

"You did what?" A frown began to deepen between Bo's eyes. "I told you I don't like the idea of you out there by yourself. What if you had been hurt? It may have been another hour before I would come over to help you. And besides that, with these roads in the shape they are right now, it may have been even longer than that before I could have gotten you to a doctor or a hospital or a mental institution." He looked at her as if he were inspecting her for damage. "I don't want you doing that again. Do you understand me?"

Gwen felt like she was facing her father who had just scolded her for doing something he felt was too dangerous for her to attempt. Her dad used to say, "This is for your own good."

"I mean it, Dallas. I know that you are feeling quite proud of yourself for doing what you did, but I have to insist that you don't try that again. I know I have no right to talk to you this way, but this is for your own good." She smiled, just thinking of those words, and then she broke into laughter. She couldn't help it. He was so serious.

"What's the matter with you? Are you nuts?" She continued laughing. "Are you crazy?"

By this time, Gwen was almost doubled over in

DONNA BARNARD

laughter. Even Pal began to wonder what was going on and started whining and pawing her leg.

At last when she could regain her composure, she said, "I'm sorry. It's just that you sounded just like my dad when you began to scold me. It sounded just like something that he would say."

Bo continued to scowl. "Well, it sounds to me that your father, at least, had enough sense to tell when something was dangerous for you. All he wanted to do was to protect you from yourself, and that's all I want to do too."

Gwen took a long deep breath to calm herself. She sighed. "You're right. I am proud of what I've done. I'm always proud of myself when I do something *for* myself. I also did it for you. I thought that perhaps I could come over here and help you do your chores. After all, you've been helping me forever. You've got to be tired of coming over every morning and every afternoon to help me do mine; and all that you ever get for it is maybe a cup of coffee, and once in a great while, you might get lucky enough to get a meal. I felt like I owed you at least helping you with your chores."

Bo smiled and rubbed his chin. "Look, I appreciate your offer. True, sometimes you are a pain in the neck; but to tell the truth, I enjoy your company. If I didn't have you to talk to, I guess I'd go crazy. Have you noticed how much company I have in a day's time? I can tell you right quick... none. I'm not much for joining, and I am really hard to get to know. I haven't made many friends since I've lived here, and you're my best friend... my only friend. That sounds awfully sad, doesn't it, but that's the fact. I made friends with your father pretty quickly, and after he died, I just had Pal,

Roxie, the horses, and the cows to talk to. As a matter of fact, I was really happy to find that you had shown up. I worry about you just like I would worry about any good friend. Not just because you're female or because I feel that you aren't capable of doing anything on the ranch. I just worry about you because I don't want you to be hurt in any way. Do you understand that?" *Yes, I understand perfectly. I am a friend—a good friend and nothing else.*

Gwen's heart was breaking, but she couldn't let Bo know. Even though she felt badly about what she had done she was angrier that Bo had made her feel that way. Gwen knew that she had to swallow her pride and make the best of the situation. "Thank you, Bo." Her voice was quaking. "I never knew just how you felt, and I'm really glad you said that. I like you too, and you are a good friend. I would like to keep being your friend. So how about this? Just to protect my pride, and yours, we'll just start doing the chores together. I'll come over and help you do yours, and you can help me do mine. How do you feel about that?"

Bo curled his lips into a dubious smile but finally said, "Okay, you have a deal." He held his hand out for them to shake. Gwen smiled. "And guess what else? I saw a panther when I was feeding." Gwen told Bo the whole story of how Apple had discovered the cat when Gwen couldn't even see it.

"Doggone it. I've wanted to see.that cat ever since I've lived here. I've heard about how the old timers call this part of the valley 'Panther Walk,' but I've just never seen the panther. You're a very lucky lady." Bo patted Gwen on the shoulder.

Gwen felt better about their feeding arrangement

because now she felt she would be doing her part. After all, she didn't want to feel obligated to Bo. She didn't know at the time how she would rue this day.

The remainder of December went by in a blur of freezing rain, freezing snow, and freezing winds. Gwen became depressed just looking out the window at the browns and grays of the Oklahoma winter, and the more she looked, the more depressed she became. Slowly January crept in. The months may have changed, but the weather remained the same. Gwen recalled reading in a book somewhere that said that the winters in Oklahoma were not all that bad. She thought probably the person who wrote that had never really spent a winter in Oklahoma.

Every day it was the same. Bo came over in the morning to help Gwen feed and hay, then Gwen would follow him back to his place and help him feed and hay; then in the afternoon Bo would come over and help put out hay, and Gwen would follow him home and help him put out hay. The humdrum days began to all blur together and were beginning to tell on Gwen's nerves. Since Christmas day, she had seen the sun a total of five days, and today was the twentieth of January. She found herself not wanting to clean house, and she began to hate the fact that she had to crawl out of bed to do chores in the dark. She hated having to get out every afternoon to do the same chores all over again. She hated the ash pan from the old stove, she hated cows, she hated horses, she hated snow, she hated cold, and she hated Bo because of his enthusiasm. Most of all, she hated herself for feeling the way she did. She couldn't help it, though. She even began to wonder about her health. She never seemed to feel well and was tired all the time. The least little chore irked her. She was being a regulation grouch, and furthermore, she was enjoying every bit of it.

Gwen knew that she was wearing on Bo's nerves also. It seemed he had very little to say when they were together, and he never stayed long when he came in for coffee after morning chores. Gwen began to miss Dallas and all of her friends. She missed the luxury of central heat and waking to a nice warm apartment in which she could take a long luxurious shower without literally freezing to death or worrying that she would run the well dry. She had started taking a shower at night only to avoid taking one in the cold of the morning. Pal was the only thing on the ranch not suffering from the winter blahs. He never changed. He was always the same and greeted Gwen each morning with an eager smile and his never-ceasing love. He would run after rabbits when she did chores and always returned happy with his tongue hanging practically to the ground. Gwen guessed that the runs kept him happy and wondered if she should begin running with him. She decided she hadn't better do that because if the ground wasn't frozen it was a bog, sucking her rubber boots from her feet.

Gwen reluctantly rose as she heard Bo's truck coming down the road and began pulling on her garb. She heard the crunch of his tires and felt a shiver. The ground was frozen again this morning. She pulled the door open and stepped out on the porch. She was met

DONNA BARNARD

by a burst of icy wind that practically forced her off the end of the porch. Bo alighted from the truck and threw his hand up. She returned a not-so-friendly greeting and started trudging out to meet him.

"Good morning," he called to her encapsulated head. "Nice brisk morning, isn't it?"

"Is that what you call this?" she answered sourly. "I call it disgusting. I have reached a point where I don't care if I ever live to see another winter. I just want this one to end. I don't like this cold. I don't mind a little cold, but this is ridiculous. I haven't seen the sun in forever, and I am really sick to death of this weather. I don't remember winters like this when I was a kid."

Gwen opened the gate, and Bo pulled through to the barn. They continued to talk as they loaded the truck from the dwindling supply of hay and feed.

"When you were a kid, you were a kid! You didn't have to get out in it and work. Your dad did all of that for you. Now it's different. You have to get out here and do what he did for all those years."

"I guess I should feel ashamed of myself, huh?" Gwen looked over at Bo, hoping he would disagree, but he ignored her question and turned to face her.

"I know what we need. We need a break. How about if we run into town tonight? Maybe we can go to a movie or something. If we wait too long, it will probably snow again, and we won't be able to get into town. And as long as we're there, we can pick up anything else we may need. I'll come over early and feed. What do you say?"

It didn't take Gwen long to make up her mind. "I say yes. I say yes, yes, yes. I have just about had it with staying in that house all the time. I am just about ready to scream." Gwen noticed herself getting excited for the first time in a long time.

"Yeah, well, I could sort of tell that you had just about had it because of your attitude yesterday."

Gwen was confused. "What about my attitude yesterday? I don't remember saying anything out of line yesterday."

"I know," he answered. "That's the problem. You didn't say anything."

She smiled. "No, I guess that isn't like me at all, is it?"

"Nope," he added while swinging into the truck. "That's not like you at all." Gwen saw a smile flicker across his face. She knew today would be a better day.

Gwen watched from the yard as Bo drove down the frozen road. She felt confused and didn't like it. She liked feeling she was in control of what was happening around her. She shrugged the feeling off and turned to the house. She felt like running, but with the old work boots on and being bundled up like an Eskimo, she thought better of it. She just smiled and proceeded into the warmth of the house.

She decided on wearing dress pants and a sweater, and since there was nothing she could do outside, she began cleaning house. Everything was dusty from wood smoke, and she needed to straighten and clean anyway. She began in her bedroom, and switched on the radio. She heard the strains of some country song being belted out by, she imagined, a blonde, buxom female. She caught herself even humming along with the music and realized that she felt happier than she had in weeks. She danced a jig across the room and wondered if Bo knew how to dance and what kind of dancer he was if he did. She imagined herself being held closely by Bo as he swung her across a dance floor and felt the blood rush to her cheeks as she thought of his arms being wrapped around her. She hugged herself and smiled. *He is nice... really nice.*

During the past winter months, there were times when Gwen felt that Bo had real feelings for her but each time she thought this, she remembered what he had said to her in his pasture. He thought of her as a friend. Gwen knew that was all she was to him, but still she wanted more. She imagined what her response would be if Bo indeed told her he loved her. She visualized the scenario but never got past his admission of love.

Shaking her head to clear it of the images and thoughts, she said aloud, "Stop that right now, girl. You have work to do, and you can't afford to let your thoughts wander... especially to that sort of thing." She started dusting again and found herself thinking the same thoughts. Her mom's words of advice came echoing into her mind. *Don't ever go out with someone you wouldn't want to spend the rest of your life with.* Gwen always wondered how she was supposed to know that if she never went out with them to begin with.

Thinking of her mother, she remembered the letter that her mom had written to her. She went into the bedroom and found it lying in the top of the cedar chest. *What was that Bible verse?* she wondered. She read through the letter again. "Hebrews 11:15," she read aloud. *Maybe the answer I need I'll find in that scripture.*

She went into the living room and picked up the Bible from the coffee table. She thumbed through it until she found Hebrews. Hiding in the pages, Gwen found another letter. Inside was a piece of notebook paper, and inside the notebook paper were ten one-hundred-dollar bills. The note inside was in Gwen's mother's handwriting.

This is for you, Gwen. I hope that you find it when you need it most.

Gwen began to cry. How long it must have taken her mother to collect this money. She had never worked and had depended on Gwen's father for everything. She found the verse and read it. *"If they had wanted to, they could have gone back to the good things of this world..."*

"Thanks, Mom. I do need this more than you know." She took the money, hugged it to her heart, and placed it in her purse. *Thanks, Mom, I needed the verse too.*

She knew now how much the ranch had meant, not only to her dad, but also to her mom. She wondered how her dad would feel about the place now and about the kind of job she was doing. She thought about how *she* felt she was doing, and thought she was doing a pretty good job in spite of it all. She had to admit to herself, though, that if it weren't for Bo she would have been lost from the first day. She thanked God for him and the fact that he had the patience to help her. She looked heavenward and whispered, "Thanks."

She checked the clock and found that the day had disappeared in cleaning and thinking. She knew Bo would be coming over soon because he had said early, and she knew what his early meant. She put the kettle on for tea and hoped she would have time for a cup. She was tired and needed to rest for a while before chores. The kettle whistled. She fixed a cup of tea and settled down in her new rocker. She pulled her feet up under her and tucked in the new afghan. She rocked her body back and forth and thought about how she had reacted to Bo's touch. She really didn't know how long sat there but was roused when she heard Pal barking. She rose, emptied her cold tea into the sink, and went to pull on her coveralls. She bent to pull on her boots. Only then did she become aware of the tears on her cheeks. She angrily brushed her face and pushed the door open. *It's just this unending winter. I know now what cabin fever means.*

Pal, of course, was waiting just outside with his ever-present smile, and Bo greeted Gwen with one to match. Gwen returned both smiles and promised herself she would be in a better humor for the rest of the day. After Gwen's chores were done, Bo pulled through the gate but remained in the truck. "You go ahead and get ready. I've already done my chores, so now all I have to do is go home and do the same. I'll see you soon." He smiled, threw up a hand in farewell, and pulled out of the drive. *So much for me helping you do your chores, Mr. Bo!*

CHAPTER SEVENTEEN

Gwen and Bo began going to town every Friday night. At least Gwen had something to look forward to. She would plan what to wear and spend time going through the cabinets and refrigerator to see what she needed; she would write a list then rewrite it.

February came at last. The groundhog saw his shadow, promising another six weeks of winter, but Gwen didn't mind because February and March always had several days of promising spring-like weather. One morning Gwen was delighted and pleasantly surprised to see jonquils. They had bloomed overnight and transformed the winter-brown yard. She picked one and breathed deeply. It smelled like spring ... at last.

Gwen made tea and, for the first time in a long time, had a glass of iced tea. She decided housework could wait and went out on the back porch to enjoy the warmer weather. While sitting in the porch swing, she noticed a cow lying about half-way between the

DONNA BARNARD

house and the foot of the mountain. The cow would raise its head, look toward its tail, then lower her head to the ground again. Several times the cow repeated this movement. Realizing what was happening, Gwen stood tiptoeing for a better look. *Oh my goodness. She's having a calf.* Gwen stood as still as stone and watched as the miracle took place. When the tiny calf was finally born, the cow began encouraging it to get up. She licked and nudged until it rose unsteadily, only fall to the ground again. "Oh no, baby. Get up," Gwen urged. She smiled as she saw the calf at last rise and begin to nurse. "Wow," she said in a quiet voice, "that was really something to see." Wiping tears from her cheeks, she walked back into the house.

With spring came the thaw and wind—lots of wind. Spring rains meant lots of mud, and then more rain, and then more mud. The pasture was acres of muck that sucked off boots and tried to swallow the truck. Gwen and Bo had to use tractors to feed.

Even though spring brought new sprigs of green grass, the two still had to feed every day. The cows eagerly chased every blade of new spring grass, but it contained no energy. As a result, many of the cows actually lost weight in the spring when they should have been gaining weight.

One morning in late March, Gwen woke to a balmy warm morning. She lay in bed and savored the new experience. Kicking the light blanket off, she rose and walked to the back door. The mountain seemed to have come to life the previous night. Beyond the stream, the trees were beginning to put on leaves and through the budding branches, and she could see a spectacular profusion of color. There were dogwoods, red bud trees, and wild plum.

Since the weather had warmed up, Bo had been talking about moving the cattle back to the summer pasture. Gwen would be sorry to see them go because she would no longer be able to see the new calves. She got a particular pleasure in watching *her* babies each day.

The feeding had practically stopped and sometimes there would be a couple of days between Bo's visits. When he did come over, they would walk through the pasture, and Bo would bend to examine the grass. "Yep, it won't be long now," he would say, indicating how long it would be until they moved the cattle. "I'm sure glad we had a wet winter. We needed it."

Early in April, Gwen got a call from J. D. Andrews, her dad's attorney. He told her that she needed to come in to the office and sign papers so he could begin making the ranch hers. Mr. Andrews said he was confident that Gwen would inherit the ranch since she only had three months left of her year's stay. At least he could get the preliminaries out of the way. The following morning, Gwen met Mr. Andrews in his office.

"We have to get a few things out of the way. No need to wait 'til the last minute." Mr. Andrews pulled a file from a jumbled pile on his desk. "Here we go," he said, pulling out a particular file on which Gwen read her father's name. "Your dad made all of the arrangements in advance. I just need you to sign some papers." He shuffled through the file until he found what he was looking for and passed several papers to Gwen. She pretended to study the papers carefully, but she trusted Mr. Andrews implicitly and after what she deemed

DONNA BARNARD

an appropriate length of time, signed the papers. She pushed them back across his desk and rose to leave.

"Thanks, Mr. Andrews. I appreciate all of your help with this. You were a good friend to Dad and now to me."

"There's one more thing, Gwen. Your dad also left you some money. I can't give it to you until your year is up, but I just wanted you to know."

"How much money are we talking about?"

"Probably around two-hundred thousand, give or take a few thousand. I haven't checked on it lately, but I imagine there's been some interest accrued in the past year."

Gwen was stunned. All she could say was, "Oh my."

"Yeah, Will made some good decisions over the years."

She extended her hand to Mr. Andrews. "Thanks again for all your help."

"Glad to do it, Gwen. Your dad and I were good buddies." Gwen could tell that the loss of her father still touched his friend.

"I'll call you when it's all done, Gwen. I'm real proud of you for doing what you've done this past year, and I know Will would be as pleased as punch. I know it hasn't been easy, but you've done a real good job. Any thoughts about what you're going to do now?"

"Not really. I've been wondering about that myself. Thanks again."

Gwen reached the door, placed her hand on the knob then stopped and turned. "Mr. Andrews, what would have happened to the ranch if I hadn't stayed here for this year? What would have become of it?"

"Why, James Bohanan, your neighbor would have gotten it."

Gwen's mouth fell open.

Bo could have been the owner of Twin Valleys if only he had let me fail. But he didn't. He helped me every step of the way. Gwen was in shock.

"Did he know that? I mean Bo—James. Did he know that he would have gotten the ranch if I failed?"

"Sure, sure. He and Will came in here together and fixed it all up. He was sitting right there when your father and he made the deal." Mr. Andrews pointed to the chair that Gwen had just vacated.

Another thought occurred to her. "Did he also know about the money?"

"No, no, no. That was just between Will and me."

"Thanks again, Mr. Andrews. I think you've just helped me make up my mind about what I intend to do."

When Gwen returned to the ranch, Pal ran to greet her. "Hey, boy. Did you protect our valuable belongings while I was gone?" She reached down to scratch him, but he backed away from her. "Hey, what's up with you? Don't want a scratch? That's a first."

She made her way to the front door, opened the screen, and looked down. Pal was whining, waiting for her to open the door. "What's wrong with you? You never want in the house unless it's freezing, and I mean fr-ee-zing." She slowly opened the wooden door, and Pal pushed his way in. "Okay, if you insist."

As she passed the picture of Christ, as was her habit, she looked up at it. She gently touched the glass. "Father," she said quietly, "now I *really* need your help." *As if I didn't before.* "Help me with this decision. I don't know what to do. I know what I would like to do, but I don't know if that's what you want of me. I wish you would help me make this decision." Off to the southwest, Gwen heard the growl of distant thunder. "Wow, that was quick." She smiled up at the picture.

Gwen didn't call Bo right away. She was going to clean house, cook dinner, and then call him to come over. Since the weather had warmed, sometimes two or three days would go by without Gwen and Bo haying, but most days Bo still found an excuse to drop by. Tonight he wouldn't need an excuse; Gwen was going to provide him with one by inviting him to dinner at her house. Gwen knew now what she had to do. She finally admitted to herself that she was in love with Bo and was going to admit it to *him* that night. *And he must love me—he gave up an entire ranch for me!* She was going to tell him tonight that she was staying on the ranch. She looked back up to the picture of Christ. "I'm staying even if he doesn't feel the same way about me. I love it here. This is my home. Thank you for helping me see that."

Gwen was well into the house cleaning, thinking about what to fix for dinner. She looked down at Pal who had not left her side since he came into the house. *Maybe he just wants some company.* She reached down to pat him on the head. "Ouch," she said, jerking her hand back, "you shocked me." She tried again, and this time he didn't cringe from her touch but whined pitifully. "Are you sick?" She continued to rub his head. She squatted down beside him. "Did you eat something that didn't agree with you? How about we open some windows; it's hot in here."

There was something different when she opened

the kitchen window, and she had to stop and think for a moment. Something was not quite right. There was a lack of sound. Birds were not singing. She propped her broom in a corner and looked out the window.

There was not a breath of air stirring, and the newly greened mountain was no longer green but a sickly yellow. The sky had yellowed too. Gwen took a deep breath. The air seemed thick and heavy. "What do you think, Pal? Are we going to have a thunderstorm?" she asked. Pushing through the back door and looking to the southwest, she saw that there was a threatening bank of clouds lying above the horizon. She noticed that although Pal always loved to be outside, he hadn't even followed her out on the back porch. Warily, she turned and went back into the kitchen where she punched the radio on. She listened only a few minutes before she heard a tornado warning. The announcement covered several counties, including hers. She and Pal went back to the window. *Maybe I should call Bo, but I don't want to appear to be an alarmist. I'll just wait for a while.* "What do you think, Pal? Should I call him now or not? I trust your judgment. No? Okay, I'll wait." She grinned at her faithful companion.

Continuing her cleaning, she soon heard thunder growling in the distance and saw streaks of lightning playing across the sky. The hair on the back of her neck began to prickle. Through the open back door, a chilly breeze began blowing. Gwen went through the house closing windows. A sudden gust of wind caught under the back porch, causing it to creak. Gwen was now concerned and decided she didn't care whether or not Bo thought she was an alarmist; she was going to call him.

She went into the kitchen and found the phone dead. "Perfect," she said, slamming the receiver down.

She grabbed her purse and pulled the truck keys out. "Pal, I'm gonna drive over to Bo's house. Do you want to come with me? He has a cellar that we can get in." She opened the door.

Pal moved toward her hesitantly then sat down.

"No? Okay. I'm going," she threatened. The dog still did not move.

"Fine, you stay here. I'm going."

Horizontal rain was blowing in the brutal winds, driving sticks, limbs, and dried grass before it. Gwen made her way to the truck and climbed in. She tried to shove the key in the ignition, but her hands were shaking so badly that she had to try twice. The truck was rocking from side to side. She turned the key and nothing happened. "Oh no. Don't do this to me now. You haven't let me down so far. Why are you doing this now?" she asked through clenched teeth. She turned the key again. Still nothing.

She jumped out of the truck and dodging several limbs and a yard chair, made her way back into the house.

Pal stood just inside the door, as if he knew she would be back.

The wind howled. Gwen still wasn't scared until she heard the roof of the house popping. She eyed the ceiling but still didn't panic. What was it that her dad had told her? Where was it she was supposed to go? *In the bathroom, get in the tub and cover your head.* "Okay, Pal. We're going to get in the bathtub. Are you ready?"

Quickly she went to the bedroom, grabbed a quilt and a pillow, and ran into the bathroom. She crawled in the bathtub and urged Pal to get in. He whined and backed up. Gwen pleaded with him. "Please get in here with me." When he finally hopped in the tub, she put the quilt and pillow over the two of them. Suddenly she remembered Apple. *Oh no, Apple! She's out in the lot; I need to go put her in the barn.* Gwen threw the quilt back, and jumped out of the bathtub. "Are you coming, boy?" she asked Pal. He only dug deeper under the quilt. "Okay. . You stay here. I have to go check on Apple." She took off in a trot.

On her way to the front door, she passed the piano and looked up at the picture of Christ. "Okay, it's me again. I really need help now for sure."

She was running to the front door when a window in the back of the living room exploded. She ran out the front door into the yard. Trees were bending to the wind. She was pelted with rocks, dust, and debris, then hail. She couldn't see where she was going and decided to run back into the house when suddenly she heard Apple whinnying. *She's afraid. I have to get to her.* Gwen was running, trying to avoid the many limbs strewn across the yard. She heard a loud crack, and a huge hickory tree fell in her path. As she turned to find a way around it, she heard Pal barking behind her. *Oh no. Pal! He shouldn't be out here.* She spun around and saw him running toward her. "Here boy! Maybe we can both make it to the barn and get in the tack room." Looking toward the barn, she saw Apple entering through the broad double doors. At least she would be in the barn. "Here, Pal!" She screamed but could not hear her own voice. Her mouth and eyes filled with dirt. Hail hit her hands hard where she held them over her head. She turned her back to the wind and closed her eyes.

Without warning, her feet came out from under her, and she was rolled violently up against the fallen hickory. Something plowed into her body but was blown over her and the tree. She forced herself to rise. She knew she had to get to Apple and the tack room. An enormous piece of lumber whizzed by her. She dodged, going one way and then the other. She looked back to see where Pal was. That was her last thought before everything went black.

CHAPTER EIGHTEEN

Slowly Gwen opened her eyes. The first thing she was aware of was pain; pain *in* her head and *on* her head. The second thing was a blur wavering before her. She heard Bo's voice. "Gwen … Gwen?" but the voice that she heard sounded very far away and resonated terribly. The pain and the blurred vision were making her nauseated. She groaned and closed her eyes again in an effort to stop the world from spiraling. Slowly she felt the nausea fading. Again she heard Bo's voice. "Gwen? Gwen?" *That can't be Bo. He's calling me Gwen.*

"Oh God, please let her be okay. Surely you wouldn't take her away from me, not after I've waited so long to find her. She's the one, Lord, and I love her so much." The words, beginning far away, were getting closer and closer. Visions of a wide ribbon of highway came drifting into Gwen's mind. She saw herself in a little red sports car, the top down, wind blowing through her hair. She was driving to a high-rise condo; she was

DONNA BARNARD

driving to a corner office. She saw herself in the front seat of the sports car. She was waving, waving good-bye ... to herself.

Then abruptly, the vision changed again. Instead of driving a red sports car, she was driving a red four-wheel drive truck, swerving to miss ancient potholes, bouncing down a country road, wind blowing through her hair, lines of clothes drying in the hot Oklahoma sunshine, children running barefoot.

Cautiously, Gwen opened one eye to test her vision and saw that the world had stopped spinning. She saw Bo's face hovering over her. He smiled and asked, "Are you okay? You were talking about a car of some kind ... and kids. Are you all right?" She nodded and a wave of nausea rolled over her. She shut her eyes again and warily rose up on one elbow; Bo extended a hand to help and placed one arm protectively across her shoulders.

"Wait just a minute, please." She sat up and looked around. Her house—the house in which she was born, was gone. All that remained of the only home she had ever known were a few stones of the foundation, and standing amidst the rubble was her mother's rosebush, proudly sporting three tiny pink rosebuds.

Surveying the damage, she noticed that the truck, her truck, was missing from the driveway. "My truck?"

"Yeah ... um, about your truck. It's halfway between here and my house. Right now it sort of looks like a pile of crumbled metal, but you can always replace a truck."

"And I know just which truck I want. I want a red, four-wheel drive," she muttered, still looking at the devastation surrounding her.

She turned too quickly to look at the barn, and her head started spinning again. She reached out to Bo, who promptly extended a hand. The barn was intact and standing in the darkened hallway; Gwen saw Apple, safe and sound, and peeking tentatively from behind her was a tiny replica of Wings. "Oh, Bo," she said, lifting her hand toward the barn, "did you see ... ?"

"Yeah, I saw it. Looks good to me."

Gwen chuckled. "We'll have to name it Tornado." *We?*

Pal ran to Gwen, gave her a doggy kiss, and other than some debris in his coat, he was fine. "You're okay," she said incredulously.

She turned back to survey the damage the tornado had wrought; slowly tears began to slip down her cheeks. "It's gone, Bo," she sobbed. "It's all gone. My home is gone." *Did I just say that? My home?*

She looked up at Bo, who had a worry frown between his brows. "Bo, why didn't you tell me about Dad leaving you the ranch if I failed? You could have had this ranch free and clear. But instead, you helped me. Why?" She decided for the moment not to mention the money.

"Ummm." He scratched his head. "Because I promised your dad."

She raised her hand and felt an enormous lump on her forehead. "Oh my goodness. I have quite a goose egg, don't I?"

"Yes, you do, and you also have a scrape on your leg ... again."

She looked back up at Bo. "I think I must have been dreaming. I thought I heard you saying that you loved

DONNA BARNARD

me. That's funny, huh?" she asked, encouragement creeping into her voice.

Bo, hearing the edge of optimism, was hopeful but reserved. "Yeah." He smiled. "That's pretty funny. I couldn't believe I was saying that, but I was. That's the other reason I helped you succeed here on the ranch. I-I love you. I've loved you since that first day we moved the cattle down here. I knew then that you were the one for me. I just couldn't figure a way to keep you here. I didn't want to encourage you to stay if you didn't really want to."

Gwen looked up into those disarming eyes.

"And don't you worry about not having a home. You'll always have a home, here—with me. If...if that's what you want. You've become quite an Okie! Yep, quite an Okie."

She turned to look at him and saw such love shining in those beautiful blue eyes, more love than she could ever have hoped to find in her lifetime. She smiled, raised her hands to his face. She turned his face so she could look him squarely in the eyes. "I love you too, Bo. I have for a long time. I just wouldn't admit it to you or to myself. T.J. was right, I am *just exactly* where God wants me to be, right here on this land and right here in your arms."

Bo lowered his lips to hers, and Gwen felt her head spinning again. But this time it wasn't because of the bump on her head.

EPILOGUE

Later that month, Bo and Gwen were married in the front yard of Bo's home, their home. They became husband and wife in the presence of God; a few friends from town including Mr. Kekso and Francine who, by the way, arrived together; T. J., Pal, Roxie, and a transplanted rose bush, which now boasted three beautiful pink roses. They've had their ups and downs over the past thirty-odd years, but that, well, that's another story.

DONNA BARNARD